The Big Burn

Also by
Jeanette Ingold

Airfield
Pictures, 1918
The Window

The Big Burn

Jeanette
Ingold

Harcourt, Inc.
San Diego
New York
London

www.HarcourtBooks.com

Although the events and some of the people mentioned
in this book are drawn from the real-life fire of 1910,
this is a work of fiction. Any resemblance of the characters
to actual people, living or dead, is coincidental.

Library of Congress Cataloging-in-Publication Data
Ingold, Jeanette.
The Big Burn/by Jeanette Ingold.
p.   cm.
Summary: Three teenagers battle the flames of the
Big Burn of 1910, one of the century's biggest wildfires.
1. Forest fires—Idaho—History—Juvenile fiction.   2. Forest fires—
Montana—History—Juvenile fiction.   [1. Forest fires—Fiction.
2. Wildfires—Fiction.   3. Idaho—History—Fiction.   4. Montana—
History—Fiction.   5. Frontier and pioneer life—West (U.S.)—Fiction.
6. United States—History—1909–1913—Fiction.]   I. Title.
PZ7.I533Bi   2002
[Fic]—dc21   2001005667
ISBN 0-15-216470-7

Text set in Caslon 540
Designed by Kaelin Chappell

First edition
A C E G H F D B

Printed in the United States of America

For my son, Kurt,
*and for all the men and women
who fight wildland fire*

The Big Burn

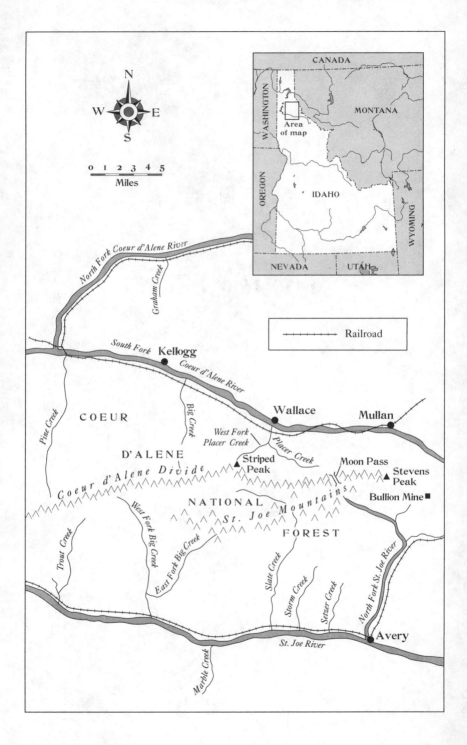

The wildfires had been burning for weeks.

They'd been born of sparks thrown from steam-driven trains and from the machinery of backcountry logging. They'd started in the working fires of homesteaders and miners and in the campfires of hoboes and in the trash-burning fires of construction camps and saloon towns. They'd begun when lightning had coursed down from an uneasy summer sky to ignite the towering snags of dry forests.

The wildfires lay behind a brown haze that was beginning to shroud mountaintops and drift like dirty fog through the forests of the Idaho panhandle. Though no one then knew it, they were fires that would join ranks and run in a vast wall of flame.

When they did, it would be called the big blowup, the great burn, the Big Burn.

Once the dead had been counted, and once the awfulness was far enough behind that people could put pretty words to what had happened, August 20, 1910, would be remembered as the day the mountains roared.

But in mid-July that year, though fire conditions were worrisome, that orange hell was still mostly unimagined as folks went about their lives.

A ranger guided a botany professor on a field trip. A peacetime soldier assembled his rifle for a training exercise. An aunt and her niece on a wilderness homestead argued about the money its timber might bring in.

And a young man went after a fire, believing fire was something he could stop.

Part

One

FIELD NOTES

A fair day followed a night brightened by dry lightning streaking to earth. Ranger William Morris set out from Coeur d'Alene Forest headquarters in Wallace, Idaho, to accompany a university professor on an expedition to look at mountain vegetation. They headed south along Placer Creek and then angled off to climb Striped Peak. A stiff wind kept them comfortable as the day heated up.

The Coeur d'Alene National Forest stretched out around them, a million and a half acres of pine and Douglas fir, of larch and hemlock and cedar. Needled treetops locked together to line canyon bottoms and cover furrowed slopes in unbroken sheets of green. In the distance, where jagged, bare peaks rose from layered tiers of rough mountains, the green turned to hazy blue.

They were eating lunch atop the sixty-three-hundred-foot summit when Morris noticed smoke in the southwest. He took a compass bearing and went back to his meal. But then a second, quickly ballooning smoke appeared in the southeast and was soon followed by the wispy track of a third fire.

He plotted their locations on his map, and then he and the professor returned to Wallace to report them.

The next time Morris climbed Striped Peak, he would find that all the land's greenness was gone, replaced by a blackened tangle of burned trees. He would write that they reminded him of jackstraws more than anything else.

Washington State
◆
July 13, Morning

Private Seth Brown, seventeen, of the all-black Twenty-fifth Infantry (except for the white officers) slid the bayonet blade onto his rifle and jammed its keyhole fitting into place. Everyone else in the squad was long done cleaning up from the morning's training and preparing for the afternoon's, but Seth—his fingers fumbling through still unfamiliar tasks—was keeping them all from going to lunch.

"Hey, Junior!" one of the men said. "You break that U.S.A. government property, and you'll be buying it out of your pay."

"Shut up," another said. "You want to slow him down more?"

Seth bent over his last task, which was to fit the required gear onto his belt for the afternoon march. He hurried as best he could, but trying to remember how to attach it all. . . . And his canteen! How could he have forgotten to fill it? Even if he didn't need the water, Sarge would notice the canteen swinging empty and get on him about that.

A hand held out a filled one, and Seth looked up to see the new guy on the squad. *Abel*, that was his name.

"I got here with an extra," Abel said, shrugging to make light of his help.

"Thanks," Seth told him. "I owe you."

"I'll collect," the other said with a smile.

Seth had seen how fast Abel had got all his own gear squared away, arriving less than an hour earlier and already fitting in. He was the kind of soldier Seth wanted to be, only the harder Seth tried, the more he seemed to mess up. Seth had thought that maybe when his company left its garrison outside of Spokane, he'd get a chance to show how he could at least stick to a hard job longer than anybody, but it hadn't happened. So far, bivouac was proving as much a disaster as anything else in the months Seth had been in the army.

Sometimes he wondered why he'd signed up—even lied about his age so he could—and then he remembered how he'd believed he could do his father proud. Join his father's old outfit and pick up where his father had left off, fighting wars and stopping riots. Those had been his father's favorite stories, told over and over those last days before sickness made his leg gangrene and then killed him.

Anger surged through Seth. It wasn't right for his father not to have told him the whole of it, how the army also meant learning a hundred new jobs and a hundred right ways to do them.

The army had a right and a wrong even for campfires, it seemed. Just that morning Seth had got up before reveille to make one, thinking the other men might welcome a way to ward off the early morning chill. Only, Sarge had yanked him to his feet and loudly demanded to know what Seth thought he was doing. "You want to burn this whole place down?"

Like I didn't have sense to handle a simple fire! Seth thought. He smarted all over again, remembering the disgusted voices of his awakened tent mates. "Brown, of course. No one else dumb enough to find trouble even before wake-up."

Now, finally, Seth attached the last item to his belt, tightened the gaiters that wrapped around his trouser legs from foot to knee, and made sure he'd buttoned the four pockets of his uniform jacket. Cut for a man, it was too full for Seth's slender body, but he couldn't do anything about that. He reached for his wide-brimmed felt hat.

"Hey, looks like you got it," the new guy, Abel, said. "Come on. Let's get some chow, and then you can tell me what's what around here."

Homestead off Placer Creek

◆

July 13, Afternoon

"Don't start," Lizbeth's aunt told her.

"You didn't buy *any*?" Lizbeth unlatched the wagon's backboard and pushed aside sacks of flour and beans in hopes they hid a roll of fencing. "Celia, you promised. You *promised.*"

"I did not. I said I would think about it on my way to town, and I did. I found nothing to change my opinion that it would be a waste of our money."

"Keeping sheep might actually *make* us some."

Lizbeth got no answer from her aunt, who was unhitching Trenton and Philly. Ridiculous names, in Lizbeth's opinion, for two hardworking horses that deserved to be called something that matched their lives. Just more of Celia's denying the realities of her and Lizbeth's wilderness homestead several miles south of Wallace, Idaho.

Lizbeth wanted to shove herself in front of Celia and make her listen, so that next spring they could put a few lambs out to forage in the forest undergrowth. Bum lambs cost practically nothing, and fattened up for a few months they'd bring in six, maybe even eight cents a pound.

But Lizbeth could tell from the way her aunt's thin face was set that explaining it all again wouldn't be any use. Celia shut her ears against any idea for making their place go.

The truth was, Lizbeth thought, Celia was scared of hearing one that might work.

Hang on. Just hang on one more year. Celia had said it so often that the words themselves hung in the air even on the days she didn't voice them. Just hang on one more year, until they got full title to their homestead and could do with it what they wanted. Once their claim was proved up, they could sell off every scrap of wood, and that was Celia's plan.

———◆———

Leaving Celia to clean up from supper, Lizbeth went out to do her chores, still seething with frustration. There were just ten years between them, Celia's twenty-six to her own sixteen. Enough of a difference for Celia to be her legal guardian, which had been Lizbeth's choice as much as Celia's, but not enough difference to keep them from arguing more like warring sisters. At least like Lizbeth imagined sisters might argue.

She chopped wood for the next day's cooking fire, hauled fresh water from the creek, and shut their rooster and five hens into the chicken house. She secured the door latch with an iron clip, something she'd been doing since the night a weasel got in and killed several chicks.

Then determined to end the evening peacefully, she

returned to the log cabin where she and Celia lived. It wasn't all that much bigger than where the chickens roosted, and, except for a horse shelter and the outhouse, it was the only other structure in the small clearing.

She found her aunt sketching guidelines for a new water-color, squinting because it was late enough that there wasn't much light coming down the lantern skylight cut in the roof. Just *skylight*, Celia called it. The way people out West talked seemed like one more thing that made Celia uneasy, their terms meaning different things from what she thought they should.

Lizbeth watched her carefully copy a magazine picture. It showed an orderly New England town where neatly dressed women visited on street corners. Lizbeth thought how different their tailored suits and large decorated hats were from her own plain gingham dress and long rough apron. Although it wasn't their clothes that set these women's lives apart from hers and Celia's as much as the way they appeared not to have things they needed to be doing. Lizbeth tucked a strand of light brown hair into the braid she wore in a loose coil above her neck.

"You know that going back, we wouldn't find it nice like that," Lizbeth said. "You married Tom Whitcomb so he'd take us away!"

"We'll find it better," Celia answered, not bothering to deny Lizbeth's accusation. They both knew the charge was true, and Tom Whitcomb hadn't deserved more. "Our timber money will see to that."

"Cel, I wouldn't want to go back if we had all the money in the world. *This* is my home, and I love it here. You would, too, if you weren't so set on closing your eyes to everything good."

"You're blocking my light," her aunt said.

"I don't want to go," Lizbeth repeated.

"You don't have a choice."

"I'll find one."

FIELD NOTES

Moisture through the winter of 1909–1910 had been close to normal, and on the Coeur d'Alene Forest, it had appeared for a while that avalanches might be 1910's worst problem.

Then, in the northern Rockies, mountain grasses barely greened up in the warmest April on record. They turned brown as a dry May gave way to a drier June and then to a July in which many weather stations reported no rain at all. The fire season roared in early. New fires began springing up daily, and the U.S. Forest Service, five years old and thinly staffed, began taking on extra fireguards and crew.

Owners of private woodland took steps to protect their interests, too. Mining and logging companies shifted their employees to fire duty when needed, and railroads hired spotters to walk the rights-of-way, where many fires started. All it took to ignite one was a lightning strike or a glowing cinder from a train's stack landing in slash left from clearing and construction.

Sometimes all it took to put one out was a man wielding a shovel—as long as he got to the fire before it grew.

Avery

◆

July 13, Afternoon

Less than fifteen miles south-southeast of the Whitcomb homestead, though a mountain divide away, Jarrett Logan was finishing the first day on his new job. At sixteen, he was younger than the railroad generally hired, but Pop had fixed it with Mr. Blakeney in the front office.

So far Jarrett had walked his assigned section of track without seeing so much as a hot cinder or glowing cigar butt to stomp out. He figured he had it easy because of how near his section was to Avery. Approaching engines were already slowing for the last bend before town, and engines leaving the rail yards hadn't gotten up to full, spark-throwing speed. Crews were careful, too, so close to where blame could be assigned and positions lost.

So when Jarrett finally smelled smoke, he was surprised. He moved quickly, anxious to find its source.

And then the wind shifted and blew stronger, and he realized the pungent odor wasn't coming from along the tracks but instead from the steep hills nearby. They weren't his to patrol, but a fire could blow down to the rail line. And if one did, by the time it got to him, it might be too big to handle.

He wished he'd asked what he should do if fire threatened from off railroad land, but he hadn't. Come right down to it, he hadn't gotten any instructions at all, except to see the right-of-way didn't catch.

With no one in shouting distance and no way to signal for help, the decision was his: go or stay.

Shouldering his shovel, he set off toward the smoke.

Twenty minutes of hard hiking and a frightening jump across a rock-filled gully took him to a low ground fire wedging up from a lightning-struck snag. A long black wound marked where the snag had been hit, and now the dead tree seemed to be burning on the inside. Smoke seeped out from jagged cracks in the wood and puffed from woodpecker holes.

It must have caught fire last night and been smoldering all day, Jarrett thought, as he tried to figure out how best to go about things. Although the ground fire didn't look to be very large, he thought that it probably posed more danger than did the burning snag, which he had no way to attack anyway. He wished the ground fire were creeping downhill instead of up, so that it might put itself out in the creek that ran just below. Shrubbery hid the stream, but Jarrett had fished its length and knew it was there.

A breath of acrid smoke set him coughing. He should have thought to ask somebody just how you *do* put out a fire when you can't get water to it. But he hadn't.

Smother it with his shovel, maybe, the same way he'd step on a spark popped out the open door of a stove.

Jarrett angled his way around one side of the fire, climbing until he was above the fire's wide, leading edge. Then he slammed the flat back side of his shovel down on low-licking flames. Nearby flames, fanned by the motion, sprang higher.

Several more swings left Jarrett with a fire angrier than the one he'd started with. Ash swirled upward, filling his nose and making his eyes water.

Frantically trying to think of something else to do, he remembered about how he always shoveled dirt over a campfire, even after he'd doused it with water. He stabbed his shovel into the ground and threw everything he dug up onto the fire. Bits of flame went out where dirt hit, but other flames glowed more brightly as they gobbled up scattered twigs and pine needles.

Next time he was careful to toss mostly soil. Then he started to work out a system. He'd scrape some earth bare and toss it and a bit of the fire's front edge farther into the blaze. *It's like folding the fire in on itself,* he thought.

By now sweat was rolling down Jarrett's face and stinging his eyes, and his arms were beginning to ache with the relentless effort of stabbing, lifting, tossing, stabbing, lifting, tossing. A wind gust blew a bunch of burning pine needles from his shovel. He glanced around but didn't see that they'd caught anything.

Stab, lift, toss. The repeated motions took on their own hard rhythm.

A deep voice yelled, "Watch your back!"

Whirling, Jarrett saw a line of flame blaze up, and all of a sudden the fire had caught him between its orange-red arms.

Other men were shouting now, and Jarrett heard tools clanging against rock and wood. He could see his way out—

just a dozen or so long steps, but running them he felt the flames closing in, flicking his neck and arms like pricks of hot knife blades. Then someone was reaching for him, grabbing Jarrett around the waist and roughly dragging him to safety. "You trying to get killed, going *above* a fire?" the man demanded.

Jarrett staggered and fell, landing hard, his elbow coming down on a boulder and taking most of his weight. Pain shot up his arm so intensely that he was afraid he'd pass out. Or maybe he did. When his spinning vision cleared, he saw that the burned area now stretched farther down, as well as up and out. The blaze appeared to be dying, though, worked by three men in miners' clothes. The nearest told him, "Go on, if you're feeling okay. We got this one."

"I'll help finish it," Jarrett said, struggling to his feet. He tried not to think about how quickly the fire had turned on him, but he couldn't help seeing the charred results of its brief run. Even the snake grass along his fishing stream was gone.

"Help's probably needed more down there," the man told him, pointing to a rose-tinged column of smoke that hung over the canyon bottom, about where Jarrett's section of rail-road track was.

———◆———

"Don't bother reporting for work tomorrow," Mr. Blakeney said, paying Jarrett off on the spot. "You're dismissed."

Trains had been held up in both directions for almost an hour while their crews fought a blaze that had threatened to burn the wood ties from under the rails. They'd barely stopped the fire from running wild through tangled, sawn trees along the right-of-way.

Jarrett tried to explain why he hadn't been on hand to see it start, but Mr. Blakeney wasn't interested. "Tell your father...," he began, and then broke off. "Tell him what you want," he finished. "It doesn't much matter, as long as you understand you're done here."

———◆———

That evening Jarrett stood alone on the north bank of the St. Joe River watching lightning streak the sky. Hardly aware of the train yard noise behind him or of the loud voices and music of Avery's bars blaring from open windows, he watched bolt after electric bolt touch down on the thickly forested hills opposite. This was the third night running he'd seen rainless clouds moving above the valley, dry thunderclouds that carried fire instead of rain.

A dot of yellow appeared partway up the nearest hill, but from Jarrett's position, it looked small and harmless.

He knew better. It probably was already mushrooming into flames like the ones that had gotten away from him and might have killed him if those miners hadn't come.

He wondered if he was crazy for wanting to go meet it. Not the particular fire he'd just seen start, but ones like it, some of them burning all across the mountains. He thought of them as *his mountains*, feeling their tug someplace deep inside him. In the months since he and Pop had moved out here, he'd come to care for this land in a way he'd never cared for anyplace or anybody. People were saying it might burn up, and this afternoon, he'd seen how. Flames rising without warning and destroying so fast.

He had to fight back, and joining a fire-fighting crew was the best way he could think of, though that would mean squaring off with Pop first.

An incoming train sounded its approach with three sharp blasts of its whistle. That would be his father's run. Inside one of the passenger cars, Pop would be telling the people whose tickets were for Avery that it was time to get off. Maybe he'd be helping a woman gather her belongings, or perhaps he'd be giving someone the correct time. Only when Pop had turned responsibility for his car over to a night-shift conductor would he retrieve his own travel valise and start for home.

Jarrett hoped Pop would be in a better mood than he was after his last run, when he'd returned still aggravated over a brakeman caught stealing tools. Of course, Pop had discharged him then and there.

Jarrett took a last look at the yellow glow in the distance, knowing that particular fire would be somebody else's to deal with. Then he started for home. He needed to put supper on the table before Pop got there. He hoped his father wouldn't have heard about the afternoon's disaster from someone else, before Jarrett could explain it his own way.

———◆———

"You can't do better than heating canned beans?" Pop demanded, ignoring the platter of corn bread and fried ham Jarrett had put on the table. He blew out a breath as though to

say food was only the beginning of his grievances. "I heard
you ran away from a fire."

"No, I missed a track fire because I'd gone to put out another one that might have spread down."

"And did you put it out?"

"I got started, but then it began moving too fast for me.
Some miners took over."

"So which was it?" Pop demanded. "You got scared off
your job, or you couldn't do it? Which do you expect me to
tell Mr. Blakeney? That you're incompetent or a coward?"

"I'm not either one. I—"

"Because he hired you on my say-so. Now what's his opinion of me going to be?"

"Why should it change? You weren't there today." Jarrett
stopped short, feeling as tangled up as arguing with Pop always made him feel. He hadn't even had a chance to bring
up his wish to take a fire-fighting job. "Look," he said, "I'm
sorry. I thought I was doing right. I didn't mean to let you
down."

He watched his father carry his half-full dish to the sink
and thump it down in disgust. Pop pulled on his jacket and
checked his beer money before swinging around where Jarrett could see his face again. "I'll go to Mr. Blakeney tomorrow morning and ask him to give you another chance. You
don't want it on your record you got fired."

"Pop, he'll say no, and anyway, my *record* doesn't matter. I
told you before I don't want to spend my life working for the
railroad."

"The day you grow up," Pop said, his eyes glittering with anger, "you're going to realize a good job with the railroad is something to be proud of."

"When I *grow up*," Jarrett said, "I'll find something more worthwhile to do than walk up and down passenger cars lighting lanterns and keeping order."

Pop stiffened. "Leave, then. You think you can find something more important to do with your life, go do it. But when you fall on your face, don't come back here."

Homestead off Placer Creek

July 13, Evening

Not ready to go inside, Celia Whitcomb leaned against the cabin's rough logs and listened to distant thunder. She hoped rain was finally on its way. It would be one less worry.

Of all the things that frightened her right now, the threat of wildfire scared her most. It was the one thing that could take her timber from her before she could sell it.

She hated feeling so helpless, watching the weather and not being able to do a thing to change it. She should have listened last spring to that old-timer. He'd said she should take the Indian way and burn while she could do it on her own terms. In the spring, burning underbrush had seemed like an unnecessary risk, but now she was considering it.

One more thing to argue about with Lizbeth, who said light burning might have been all right in April, when melting snow was still running down from the mountains. But, Lizbeth said, in the middle of a dry July they might as well throw flaming torches into the woods.

Lord knows Celia hated arguing with her niece, but it

seemed that's all they did these days. Maybe because Lizbeth was so much like she herself used to be, thinking she could mold the world to her liking. When Celia's sister had died, leaving twelve-year-old Lizbeth an orphan, Celia hadn't hesitated to take her in.

But then the girls' school where Celia was working closed, and no other nearby school needed a female art teacher good at penmanship and simple arithmetic. Tom Whitcomb had seemed like a blessing, sweeping in with promises he'd take care of her and her niece. "We'll go out West," he said, "where people become rich just by living. You claim a forest homestead, prove it up, and five years later sell the timber for a small fortune."

Celia had said, "But if we need to clear the land for crops as part of proving up, then we won't have timber left to sell."

How he'd laughed. "We'll put in a garden just big enough to say we did. Maybe, along with a cabin, it'll take two acres out of the hundred-sixty acres I can claim. And, of course, we'll put you in for another hundred-sixty in your own right."

By the time she learned that making people rich off timber wasn't the intent of the homestead laws, Celia was in the land office in Wallace, Idaho, officially Mrs. Tom Whitcomb.

Tom Whitcomb had stayed around just long enough to build the poorest excuse for a house that would pass for the required improvement, and then he'd taken off on the first of his many absences.

And Celia, alone with Lizbeth in a wilderness canyon, a long ride from town and other settlers, was left with lots of time to figure out where she'd gone wrong. She decided it must have been when she agreed to leave New England, and so gradually she fixed it in her mind that going back was the only thing to do.

Tom Whitcomb's accidental death—if getting so drunk he drove a team of horses over a cliff could be called that—had just left her more determined. Of course, the government took back the hundred-sixty acres that he'd claimed and not lived long enough to get the patent on, but Celia still had her own land. A quarter of a square mile of the most beautiful white pine and larch growing anywhere. At today's prices it would fetch maybe even ten thousand dollars.

Enough to return East and live for years on, and Lizbeth with her as long as her niece wanted. Although, Celia supposed, once Lizbeth began living like a young lady instead of like a farmhand with tanned skin and muscled arms, suitors would come swarming. Goodness knows, Lizbeth's fine-boned features and dark eyes made her pretty enough, even if Lizbeth herself didn't seem to know it.

The only thing Celia hadn't foreseen was Lizbeth's mistaking this place for a permanent home.

That, and the possibility of fire coming through. Celia had tried to put it from her mind, but there was no ignoring either the superdry ground or the rainless lightning these recent nights had brought.

A shooting star arched overhead, reminding her of how Halley's comet had trailed through the sky a few months earlier. Some had said it portended the coming of glory, and others had said it was an omen that something bad lay ahead—very bad.

Maybe tomorrow she'd again talk to Lizbeth about their starting some small burns to get rid of underbrush that would be fuel in a wildfire. If she kept calm, maybe for once she could make her niece see reason.

Cool Spring Ranger Station
July 13, Evening

In the yellow light of a kerosene lamp, Ranger Samuel Logan looked at the small photograph of his parents. It showed his father, straight backed and proud in his railroad uniform, standing beside Samuel's seated mother.

If he remembered right it had been taken two or three years after his brother, Jarrett, was born, and before Mother's sickness had taken full hold. Not much later, Samuel had left home. Leaving was the first and only time Samuel had ever defied Pop and got away with it. He'd wanted to work in the woods, instead of for the railroad. He'd been fifteen, old enough to do odd jobs at one of the lumber camps that dotted Minnesota.

His mother, thin and fragile as a blade of alpine grass, had swayed before the force of Pop's anger but taken Samuel's side. "It's Samuel's decision, Mr. Logan," she'd said. That's what she called her husband: *Mr. Logan*, not *Ian*, and to this day, Samuel would lay good money Pop had never asked for different. "You can't decide Samuel's calling for him."

When she died the next year and Samuel returned for her funeral, it seemed to him that Pop believed her death had somehow proven Pop right in a long-running disagreement. There was no hint of grief in his unforgiving face. Or of welcome for Samuel.

Samuel had never gone back again.

And now, just this morning, he'd learned from an angry exrailway worker that Pop and probably Jarrett were living in Avery, a few hours' ride away.

The man had been applying for a job with the Forest Service when Samuel had checked in at the Wallace office. The man picked up on the Logan name and probably on how closely Samuel resembled his father, with his bushy hair the color of red sand and the height that made Samuel tower over everyone. "If you're related to the Logan conductoring out of Avery," he said, "you tell him to watch his back. Twenty years I was with the railroad, and he fired me for one slipup and blacklisted me, too."

Studying the man's shifting, belligerent gaze, Samuel had guessed there'd been more than just one slip, though that was not his worry.

So, Samuel thought now, *the question is, Do I get in touch? I could ask one of the men at the ranger station down there to go look them up for me.* Even though Samuel still had no wish to see Pop, he would like to know that Pop was okay.

And Jarrett was a different story altogether. Nearly a stranger, but also Samuel's only brother.

It was just unfortunate he'd got news of them right at this time. Samuel didn't need a distraction when he had his hands full trying to keep fire off the thousands of acres he was responsible for.

FIELD NOTES

Perhaps the ancients had it right, honoring and giving the keeping of fire to gods and goddesses—to Rome's Vesta, India's Agni, the Greeks' Hephaestus. Fearing its mighty power for destruction when it trailed the horsemen of the Apocalypse.

Now we understand fire as chemistry. We know it to be combustion, a chemical change that occurs when oxygen combines with another substance. Fire requires the presence of heat to get started. But then fire is combustion happening so fast that the reaction itself causes heat and light to burst forth.

Only, that's like defining people as composites of water and minerals, without mentioning the life inside them. Life that requires air to breathe and food to eat, and that has a mysterious soul at its core.

To stay alive a person needs air that's about 21 percent oxygen, and that's about what a fire needs, too. Rob fire of the air around it and it dies.

And just as a person can be killed by starvation, so can a fire be killed by depriving it of fuel.

Two facts—a fire can't start without heat, and a fire can't keep going without oxygen and fuel—are all any firefighter has to work with. Those, and a harbored respect for the capricious life inside flame.

Avery

July 14, Morning

Jarrett had lain awake most of the night, scared at what he was setting out to do. Scared that he didn't know what he was getting into, volunteering to fight fires that might be measured in miles instead of fractions of an acre. Scared that Pop might know him better than he knew himself. Jarrett didn't think he was a coward, but how could a person know that for sure until the time came to prove it?

That remark Pop had made about how Jarrett needn't come back—Jarrett guessed he shouldn't have expected anything else, but until he heard it said, he hadn't realized just how final his leaving would be.

When morning came, though, he shoved aside his qualms. He put together traveling food, wrapped spare socks and an extra shirt in a blanket, and put two dollars on the table to pay for what he was taking. It left him with only pocket change, but he'd have gone with no money at all before he'd have taken off without setting things square.

He found the ranger station on its hillside perch above town already busy, even though it was still early. Men wearing

Forest Service badges gave him a real welcome when he said he'd come for a job. One told him, "We were just talking about putting together a fire crew to send over to Big Creek." He pulled out a hiring log and dipped a pen in an inkwell. "Name?"

"Logan. Jarrett Logan."

The man looked up in surprise and then said, "I should have guessed it from that mop of rusty hair." He put down the pen and reached for a paper. "This message about you just got relayed down."

Jarrett struggled to take in the words he read while the man went on talking. Finally Jarrett asked, "And you're saying you know my brother? That he's a ranger and living near Wallace?"

"That's right. He's got the Cool Spring Station."

The others were also looking at Jarrett curiously now. "Funny you didn't know," one said.

"I . . . we lost track of him years ago," Jarrett said, wondering if his face showed how his mind was reeling.

The men took it as natural that Jarrett would wish to visit his brother before doing anything else. "Hate to lose you here," the man at the desk told him, "but if you still want to fight fires, you can get on in Wallace. That's where forest headquarters are anyway."

"I'll remember," Jarrett said.

———————◆———————

The route north took him through the blackened area where he'd failed so badly at his job, and then into country he hadn't explored. For the first several miles, he followed rail

bed carved into mountainsides high above the St. Joe
River's north fork. Where the steep hills flattened into narrow benches, he slowed to look at the maintenance shacks
and tiny houses that were squeezed into every available
space. Spare rolling stock—crane and dump cars, shop cars
and a snowplow—took up siding tracks that curved close to
sheer drop-offs.

Where the railroad spanned the canyon, he saw teams
hauling earth fill for trestle bridges that were still so new their
wood hadn't weathered. He stopped for a while to watch a
crew bolting together huge timbers to make a snow shed at
the end of a tunnel.

Then, to make up time, he cut through a tunnel instead of
going around. Midway in, the rough-sided vault curved and
shut out light, and Jarrett had to feel his way along wet rock.
And then, at the tunnel's far end, he and a train came dan-
gerously close to meeting, and the engineer leaned on his
whistle in a long blast of reproach.

Jarrett's heart pounded hard a good while after that.

He ate supper where the railroad tracks veered east to the
Idaho-Montana border. Then he started up the trail that
climbed north to cross the divide at Moon Pass. By then Pop
and Avery and just about everything else Jarrett had known
already seemed far more than a day's hike behind him.

He spent the night high in the mountains at Moon Pass,
watching dry lightning in the distance and thinking about
what lay ahead.

He wondered what kind of man he'd find his brother to
be. Surely Sam couldn't be as worthless and irresponsible as

Pop maintained and still hold down a job as a ranger. "He's gone and good riddance," Pop used to answer, back when Jarrett still asked why Sam had left.

    Jarrett thought about the fire-fighting job that was still his main aim. He hoped he'd be good at it.

FIELD NOTES

They were called the buffalo soldiers. The name was a proud one, given to the black cavalrymen and foot soldiers who manned territorial forts and fought the Indian wars. One historian computed that if you met trouble in the days of the Wild West and the military rescued you, there was a one-in-five chance your rescuer would be black. He might have been one of the eighteen buffalo soldiers who would, before 1900, earn Medals of Honor. Once he was done saving you, he'd have gone back to a dusty adobe or log fort, where he'd likely have hauled water, chopped wood, pulled guard duty, or hoed a vegetable garden.

With the Indian wars a memory, the buffalo soldiers moved on to other duty. In the early 1890s the black soldiers and white officers of the Twenty-fifth Infantry brought order to labor strikes in the Northwest. Some of them made newspaper headlines in 1897 when their experimental bicycle corps pedaled from Montana to St. Louis, drawing crowds and cheers.

As the century closed, the Twenty-fifth's soldiers carried their flag—dark blue background, a fierce eagle—on campaigns in the Philippines and Cuba. Back home again they patrolled the borders between the United States and Mexico. They were jolted when racial strife escalated and a 1906 shooting incident in Texas ended in 167 of them being summarily discharged. They rallied for another stint in the Philippines.

In 1909 the Twenty-fifth returned to take up garrison in Washington State, and in July 1910 the regiment's various companies left their barracks for maneuvers at summer training camp at American Lake, south of Seattle. By then citizens frightened by spreading forest fires were beginning to ask for the military's help.

◆

The buffalo soldiers varied in the skills and hopes they brought to the army. Many couldn't read, but that was true across the enlisted ranks then. Some would learn, taught in army classrooms. Some would come to care deeply for the service and make long careers of it. Others would desert, although the desertion rate among black troops was substantially lower than in white units, and morale was often higher.

The men of the Twenty-fifth came from many backgrounds, but most had been born in the rural South. The army offered a way out from lives of endless farmwork, often on fields they didn't own. The soldiers looked to the army for adventure, steady pay, and dignity.

Washington State

July 15, Morning

"Burn, baby!" Abel said, moving a lighted match along heaped trash. He jabbed a rake into the pile and stirred it up.

"Hey, careful!" Seth told him, as a gusty breeze carried off ashy bits of paper. Seth chased after a newspaper sheet, causing Abel to laugh. "What's so funny?"

"Just you running your scrawny tail off for nothing."

"But we just got done policing up, and now stuff's blowing all over."

"Seth, buddy," Abel said, "no one's looking. It ain't blowing back to *our* company area, and that's all we got to see to. That and getting done here without taking all day."

Abel was right, Seth thought, as they stood at attention. The corporal was happy because their squad had been the first lined up for inspection. Sarge, walking beside a lieutenant, appeared pleased, though no smile broke the military set of his charcoal-dark face.

And when the inspection broke up, Sarge even mentioned

how good the company area looked. "The new man's doing,"
the corporal said. "His and Brown's."

"If they're a good team," Sarge said, "keep them together."

———◆———

"Cards later on?" Abel asked Seth, coming into their tent.
"Some of the guys are getting up a game."

"Prob'ly not. I'll still be getting ready for tomorrow." Seth
was using the free minutes before lunch to clean his second
pair of shoes.

"Toss me one of those," Abel told him. "We can get you
done."

"Besides," Seth said, "that card game's been going on for
weeks, and ain't anybody said anything to me about playing."
He grew embarrassed under Abel's sharp gaze. "I ain't much
good at mixing in."

"How do you know? You can't just wait around to be
asked."

Though that's where Abel proved wrong. In the mess tent,
one of their tent mates hailed them. "Abel! Junior!" he
called. "Here's seats."

Seth couldn't remember that happening before, his fitting
into any army place that easy.

Cool Spring Ranger Station

◆

July 15, Afternoon

Near Placer Creek, on the Wallace side of the Coeur d'Alene divide, Jarrett strode into a forest clearing where an American flag flew at the peak of a log cabin. A huge, barking German shepherd ran out and took a menacing stance between Jarrett and the building. Jarrett halted and yelled, "Hello!"

It appeared that Sam, or at least someone, was around. A cabin window stood open, and a harness and some leather-working tools had been left by a rocking chair on the porch. A couple of axes leaned against a grindstone mounted on a three-foot-wide stump.

Jarrett was near enough the building to read posters nailed up beside the front door. One of them, made on a printing press, said WARNING: PROPERTY OF THE UNITED STATES GOVERNMENT. The other notice, hand-lettered, read Wife Wanted. He guessed the second must be a joke.

"Hello!" he yelled again, causing the dog to break into a fresh round of barking.

Someone whistled from the direction of the corrals, and a firm voice called, "Boone! Stand down!"

The broad-shouldered man who walked out to greet Jarrett looked so much like Pop that Jarrett took an involuntary step back. Jarrett had expected the Logan hair, but Sam also had Pop's wash-blue eyes and bushy mustache. He'd be twenty-eight now—Jarrett had figured that out on his trip up from Avery—but he seemed to wear authority as though he were older.

"Jarrett," he said, making it a statement. He put out a hand to shake.

"Sam."

"I go by Samuel now."

For a moment it seemed to Jarrett that maybe they'd just said all they had to say to each other. Then he managed, "The people in Avery told me you're a ranger."

"That's right."

"I met them when I went to sign up for fire fighting."

"Yeah. They said." Samuel seemed stuck for talk, too, until he asked, "You hungry? Thirsty?"

"Not really," Jarrett answered, beginning to wish he hadn't come here. "Thanks anyway." This man really *was* a stranger. "I just stopped by... I mean, I'm my way up to Wallace..."

Samuel's eyes flickered amusement. "And you don't have time for a cup of coffee?"

———◆———

While Samuel heated water, Jarrett looked around the main room of the station, where his brother apparently lived as well as worked. Samuel had put bearskins on the floor and moose antlers on the walls. Stuffed birds and piled-up books and a framed photograph that Jarrett recognized as his parents filled a shelf. By a curtained-off doorway that probably led to a bedroom, a telephone, a tacked-up map, and a desk stacked with papers formed an office area.

"I didn't guess you'd have a telephone out here," Jarrett said.

"It's new," Samuel said. "This is one of the first stations to get one."

"You like it?"

"It's a change."

Along the opposite wall, where Sam—*Samuel*, Jarrett reminded himself—was working, a sink with a hand pump, a woodstove, and a screen-covered pie chest made a kitchen.

A round table, a few wooden stools, and a comfortable-looking reading chair took up pretty much the rest of the room. Samuel pushed aside scrapbooks to make space for coffee mugs, and then he set out a box of crackers. He said, "I've never been much for cooking, and these days, with fires acting up all over, I'm too busy to do any at all."

"Crackers are fine," Jarrett said.

The talk bumped along as the two of them felt each other out.

Samuel asked, "And how have things gone for you?"

"Not much to tell," Jarrett answered. "After Mother died, Pop and I moved around the Midwest with his transfers. Then after the Milwaukee line pushed through the St. Joe, Pop took a senior job when one opened up in Avery. He even bought a house."

"Up till then you were still boarding?"

Jarrett nodded.

Samuel looked away. "Pop ever remarry?" he asked, his voice flat.

"No."

"So how is he?"

"You're asking someone too mad at him to give a fair answer. The way I see it, all he thinks about is his railroad job, and how everybody else's work is to see he gets to do his."

Samuel laughed without sounding as though he found Jarrett's statement one bit funny. "Yeah, that always was his take. How'd you get him to let you come up here?"

"I didn't tell him."

Samuel's eyebrows rose. "Unless Pop's changed, you're in for a bad time when you go home."

"I'm not going back," Jarrett said. "I already told you, I'm heading into Wallace to sign on a fire crew." Jarrett fiddled with the crackers, buying time while he turned over a half-formed idea. "Unless, of course, you need a hand here? I want to help out in the forests, but I don't care *which* forests."

When Samuel didn't answer immediately, Jarrett quickly said, "Never mind. I'll sleep here tonight, if that's okay, and then head to town in the morning."

"Sure," Samuel said. "Headquarters will be glad to get you."

◆

It wasn't until hours later, when Jarrett was carrying his blanket up to the cabin's half loft, that Samuel asked, "You know how to ride a horse?"

"Yes."

"Because I was thinking, if you want, you can ride patrol

with me tomorrow. Maybe help me with trail work that needs doing, and we can see how things go." Samuel handed up a pillow. "Of course, I couldn't put you on the payroll, at least not till I can get to town and okay it there."

"No matter about the money," Jarrett answered. "I wouldn't have anything to spend it on anyway." He paused. "You don't have to do this."

"I can use the help."

"Because I don't want make-work," Jarrett said. "If the fire danger is really as bad as everybody's saying, I want to be doing something that'll make a difference."

"The danger is that bad," Samuel answered, "and the worse it gets, the more important patrol becomes."

FIELD NOTES

Someone who knows the signs can read the history of a land in thin layers of charcoal buried in soil. The story lies in the maturity of tree stands, in blackened patches called cat-faces hollowed into bark, in the kinds of grasses that grow, and in the fuel available to feed the next fire. A forest fire leaves signs that can be read decades later.

People moving into the Northwest in the late 1800s and early 1900s looked at what had once been Indian land and saw that fires had moved through it time and again. The newcomers came to two different conclusions.

Some—especially settlers accustomed to fire being as much a tool as their plows and hammers—looked at hundred-year-old trees growing in recently scorched ground and said perhaps the Indians had known what they were doing, setting fires annually when the seasons were right. Such light burning, they said, not only opened up forage land for game animals and encouraged the growth of desirable plants like berry bushes, it also got rid of unwanted fuel before it could build up to feed unfightable wildfires.

Others—most others—looked at blackened hillsides and concluded that the only safe way to control fire was to not let it burn in the first place.

The professional foresters of those early days sometimes used fire against itself, but they didn't trust it. They might battle a wildfire by lighting another fire—a backfire—to consume fuel the wildfire would need. They might widen an encircling fire trench by burning a black line alongside its inner edge. But, regardless of whether they occasionally enlisted fire's help, most early foresters belonged to the faction that believed fire was primarily an enemy to be vanquished.

The differing views caused dissension, but the foresters who thought fire was best abolished had law and regulation on their side.

Homestead off Placer Creek

July 16, Morning

"Cel, we don't have to do this," Lizbeth said. "We *shouldn't* do it."

"After all the work we did getting ready?" her aunt demanded.

Lizbeth felt like saying, *And I told you that was dumb.* She bit back the angry words. After all, once she'd let Celia talk her into preparing an area where they could experiment with brush burning, she'd thrown herself into the effort as though it had been her own idea.

Celia had said that if Lizbeth wouldn't help, she'd do it alone. *And really burn the place up*, Lizbeth had thought.

Between them they'd cut away low limbs and small shrubs to clear two narrow firebreaks twenty feet apart, running from a gravel face on the edge of their property down a hundred feet to a small stream. Celia's idea was to carefully burn the underbrush between the breaks, with her working one side and Lizbeth the other to keep the fire from spreading.

Now, seeing the inadequate barriers in the pale light of predawn, Lizbeth renewed her arguments. "This might have been okay in the spring, before the weather turned so hot and dry, but—"

"That's why we're out here this early," Celia answered. "The morning cool is on our side." She pulled out a match. "We'll start small, and we'll keep it small," she promised again. "Just do this section today, and if it goes the way I think it will, then we'll start on another tomorrow. You ready?"

Lizbeth picked up a shovel. "Not too late to change your mind..."

But her aunt was already holding the lighted match to a clump of weeds. For a moment the parched blades blackened without igniting, and then the grass took, and then a small bush caught, and another.

Lizbeth and Celia flapped gunnysacks and used their shovels to herd the blaze, carefully driving it before them, leaving black ground behind. Lizbeth worked with her skirt tucked up high, heat piercing the soles of her shoes and her heart beating wildly. It seemed impossible that this was working.

And then, when they'd almost reached the stream, the fire jumped and caught the shoulder-high branches of a young cedar. "Use water!" Lizbeth shouted, running ahead to wet down her gunnysack and then back to beat at the flames with the soaking cloth. Somehow, between them, she and Celia quenched the blaze just when it seemed about to stretch beyond reach.

Meanwhile, the ground fire had gotten to the creek and was threatening to jump over. Only the water slowing the fire's advance allowed the women to put out the flames.

Then they sank to the ground, faces bright red and chests heaving. The scare they'd come through had left Lizbeth so angry she couldn't find words strong enough to throw at her aunt. She knew the two of them were plain lucky they hadn't burned the whole forest down.

Celia pointed her chin at the sky as though she was mad at God himself for threatening her trees. "Whatever you're thinking to say," she told Lizbeth, "I don't want to hear it."

Cool Spring Ranger Station
July 16, Morning

Jarrett, finishing a breakfast of cold biscuits, bear jerky, and eggs, watched Samuel pin on his ranger badge. "Want me to pack grub for the day?" Jarrett asked.

"For two days," Samuel answered, putting on his brimmed ranger's hat and feeling for the fishhook in its band. His badge and pistol, and that hat, with its crown peaking over four precise dents, seemed to be his only uniform. "Don't dawdle. I want to be riding by dawn."

Jarrett gathered up canned beans, canned tomatoes, and the last of the biscuits he'd made the night before. His brother had been grateful for the biscuits, saying they went a long way to improving the taste of bear. "I can't see wasting meat when I got to kill any animal," he'd said, "but some kinds do seem to last forever."

Outside, Jarrett helped him strap shovels, axes, and a two-person saw onto a pair of packhorses. They also loaded up newspapers, a rake, and a sack of flour to drop off at various homesteads. "Is that part of your job?" Jarrett asked.

"No, but it eases the part that is," Samuel answered. "As

far as homesteaders are concerned, I'm the law, which, alone, isn't always so welcome."

Samuel saddled his riding horse, a large sorrel gelding named Thistle, and Jarrett rounded up a little black mare for himself. She was the last horse remaining in the corral.

By then Boone was circling, eager to get going, and when the two brothers finally were ready, the dog led off, his head up and his nose taking in all the scents on the early morning air.

Jarrett thought he knew just how Boone felt. He was pretty excited himself.

———◆———

They rode first to a lookout tree on a high point a couple of miles from the ranger station. It was just boards nailed to the trunk of a ponderosa pine to make a ladder. Jarrett held the animals while Samuel climbed up. "No new smokes that I can see," he called down, sounding satisfied.

From there they put in ten miles before lunch, stopping to chop brush and roll boulders from the trail. They delivered some of the items they'd brought settlers, and at one place they stopped long enough to help a homesteading couple lift a heavy wheel onto a wagon axle.

"That part of earning your welcome, too?" Jarrett kidded as they rode away.

"Just turnabout," Samuel answered. "Come a fire, I'll need all the neighborhood men to help fight it."

———◆———

After lunch came more of the same, except that one of their stops was at a hard-rock mine. Samuel asked the owner how he was fixed for handling fires.

"I have my men taking turns on fire watch," the owner answered, passing Jarrett and Samuel mugs of boiled coffee.
"And a good thing. Just yesterday we stopped a blaze that
might have turned nasty."

"Lightning strike?" Samuel asked.

"Picnickers on a fishing outing, if you can believe that. You
ask me, Idaho ought to pass a law against fools." They all
laughed, and the mine owner took the lid off a tin box.
"Pound cake?"

"Thanks," Samuel said. "My brother here's been questioning the point of my patrol work. Now he can see it's 'cause
I get fed better than I eat at home. Right, Jarrett?" Then
Samuel turned serious again. "You have a plan in case wildfire comes this way?"

"Besides fighting it?"

"If you got trapped," Samuel answered. "Not that I expect
it to happen. I'm just asking, What if?"

"I suppose the mine tunnel would give shelter," the man
said, glancing toward the timbered adit where Boone had
settled in a patch of damp shade. "I doubt a fire would burn
so hot we couldn't survive in there."

"Be hard to imagine one," Samuel agreed.

———◆———

As they rode away side by side, Jarrett asked his brother,
"How come you wanted him to have an escape plan if you
didn't think he'd need one?"

"Because worst-case planning never hurts, and out here it
just might save your life."

"You know that from experience?" Jarrett asked. Then,

looking sideways, he saw Samuel's eyes narrow as though at some painful thought, and he wished he hadn't spoken.

"I know it from friends who never learned." Leaning forward in his saddle, Samuel turned to look at Jarrett more directly. "You promise me you'll remember that. If you ever do get in a firefight, the first thing you do is figure out how you'll get out if things go bad."

"Sure," Jarrett answered, a little scared by the intensity in his brother's voice.

Samuel faced ahead again. "Because folks don't, and that's when they get killed. You got to think what a fire might do. If it's likely to run up a hill or stall at a ridgeline. If it's reaching into a canyon that can turn into an inferno in minutes. And then you got to see you don't get caught."

Jarrett absently wound the ends of his mare's reins around the saddle pommel, unwound them, and finally blurted out, "That doesn't sound very brave."

"And that's what you're here for?" Samuel asked. "To prove how brave you are?"

"No, I—"

"Because anybody who works for me better understand they take care of their men first, themselves next, and the forests last. And I say that even though I love these forests better than anything in the world."

The talk embarrassed Jarrett, both how he'd sounded shallow and how Samuel had exposed his feelings, and he was glad when they came on a downed tree big enough to demand their attention. Lying right across the trail, it was too heavy to move, so Samuel decided they'd use their two-man crosscut saw to go through it twice. "Then we can push away the middle section."

"Why don't we ride around?" Jarrett asked, halfway into the first cut. His saw arm was tiring, and he reached down to pet Boone while he rested it. "I think we could get through."

"Maybe," Samuel answered, "but the forest is thick enough in here that a heavily loaded pack string would have trouble. The main reason to maintain trails is so when fire breaks out, we can move men and supplies around quickly."

They were into the second cut when Samuel suddenly asked, "So, just why *did* you decide to leave Avery?"

"I messed up a job I had spotting fires for the railroad."

"So bad they wouldn't give you another chance?"

"Probably not, and anyway, I wouldn't have taken it. Maybe you'll laugh, but I wanted to do more to take care of the woods than just walk the train tracks and look for cigar butts. That's why I figured to take a fire-fighting job, only then I read your message and sort of detoured . . ." Jarrett's voice trailed off.

"I'm not laughing," Samuel replied, "although when it comes to fighting forest fires, it's hard to beat putting out a fire before it gets a decent start."

"So you don't think I was right to leave?" Jarrett asked, smarting at how, no matter what he said, Samuel seemed to find some way to twist it into a mistake that needed correcting. It was like talking with Pop, although at least Samuel's lessons made some sense. Jarrett pulled on his end of the saw. "Are we going to get this job done?"

When the saw had traveled its length, Samuel drew back

his end. "I imagine the railroad will survive without you," he answered. "But it does worry me you left Pop by himself."

It was the last thing Jarrett expected to be faulted on. "Me! You're the one who left first. You left all of us."

"Maybe I was wrong."

Jarrett struggled to keep his voice from shaking. "That's fine for you to say, now that you've done what you wanted these last dozen years. Anyway, Pop wants to be alone. He told me not to come back."

"He might not have meant it."

"I tell you, he doesn't care!" Jarrett jerked his end of the saw so savagely that the blade twisted and stuck. "Right now he's probably saying good riddance to me, just like he says it about you." Jarrett looked up quickly and saw that Samuel's face had flushed scarlet. "I'm sorry. I shouldn't have said that."

"The way I see it," Samuel said, "I didn't walk out on an aging man who might have needed me. You did."

Jarrett concentrated on working the saw blade free. "I doubt the day comes Pop will ever need anyone. If you don't want me here, just say so, but don't think I'll go back to Avery, because I won't."

———◆———

Samuel brought the matter up only once more, late in the afternoon during his first check of a drainage that had recently been added to the area he was supposed to look after. He said, "I've no right to tell you what to do outside your job here, if that's what it turns into. As long as you do your work right, you're welcome to stay."

He pulled up Thistle and motioned Jarrett to halt. Boone had stopped dead center in the trail, his whole being on full alert.

"What is it, boy?" Samuel asked. He sniffed. "Jarrett, you smell scorching?"

"I don't smell anything different from the smoke that's been with us all day," Jarrett answered.

Samuel lightly tugged Thistle's reins to the right. "I think it's coming from the other side of that ridge."

They crested a low rise and found themselves above an expanse of gravel. Below it, blackened undergrowth stretched down to a small stream. Leaving Thistle for Jarrett to hold, Samuel walked down to explore the burn, burrowing into it with his hands, smelling and frowning. "Still warm, but I didn't find hot spots," he said, coming back.

Jarrett didn't understand why his brother seemed angry instead of relieved that the fire was out. "Then what's the matter?"

"Someone set this."

"How can you tell?"

"By the shape of it. By those two firebreaks somebody cut." Samuel swung into his saddle and snapped the reins. "Come on."

Homestead off Placer Creek

◆

July 16, Afternoon

Lizbeth spotted a dog and two riders approaching. The late afternoon sun glinted off a shiny badge on the larger one's shirt. "Celia," she said, "there's a ranger coming." The words were the first she'd spoken to her aunt since they'd returned to the house.

"You must be wrong," Celia said, going to the window. "Oh, goodness. Do you think they found our burn?" She hurried out to reach the newcomers before they could get off their horses, and Lizbeth, following on her heels, heard her aunt say, "We've already been checked for this year. Another ranger came through in the spring and saw we were here doing our six months and a day."

"And you are . . . ?"

Celia answered, "I am Mrs. Tom Whitcomb."

"Then I reckon I need to see Mr. Whitcomb," the ranger said.

"I'm a widow. If you have a question about this land, you may take it up with me."

Why in the world, Lizbeth wondered, *does Cel have to get so high-and-mighty? She's just going to make matters worse.* Lizbeth moved around to where she could give her aunt a private poke in the back.

Uninvited, the ranger got down off his horse. The person with him—a boy who looked about Lizbeth's age—dismounted also, and tied his mare and two packhorses to a corral rail. Lizbeth saw him glance swiftly about.

"Looks like somebody's been burning brush," the ranger said. "That you folks?"

"Only some light burning," Celia answered, making it sound like an activity everybody just naturally did.

"Season's past for that."

"Is it?"

Lizbeth didn't dare look at her aunt, since she knew quite well Celia had been aware of that fact.

"You need a permit to burn, and they're not issued for the middle of the summer."

The ranger was sounding a lot more reasonable than his unflinching expression said he wanted to be, Lizbeth thought, and she hoped her aunt would have the sense not to argue.

"And just who decides the permit period?" Celia demanded. "You?"

"The Forest Service," the ranger answered. The back of his neck had turned red. "And the state."

"And just who is that? Some bureaucrat who doesn't own a stick of timber? I suppose you don't own any either, because if you cared two figs about these woods, you'd see they need protecting!"

Cel, Lizbeth wanted to say, *shut up before he slaps a fine on us or hauls us off to jail.*

She suddenly wondered if the ranger might even have the

power to take away Celia's land claim, if she broke the rules. She cast about for a way to stop her aunt before Celia pushed him into a corner he'd have to fight out of.

A little desperately, extending her hand to the ranger's companion, she said, "I'm Lizbeth, Mrs. Whitcomb's niece. We've got a fresh berry pie and coffee in the house. Would you and the ranger like some?"

Maybe it sounded silly, given the hard words just spoken, but it was all she could think of. And it did startle the others into silence.

"Sure, thanks," the boy finally managed, though he stared at her hand another long moment before apparently figuring out he was supposed to shake it. "Pie and coffee would be great. Great." He paused. "I'm Jarrett," he added. "Jarrett Logan. I'm Ranger Logan's brother. That's him. Ranger Logan. Samuel. My brother."

◆

Leading the others inside, Lizbeth tried to see the cabin through the Logan brothers' eyes. She was so used to it that most of the time she didn't notice how cramped it was. Now she wished there was more than one room, so at least the pole bed she and Celia shared would be out of sight.

And she wished that the platform they had hanging on wires from the roof was higher up, so Ranger Logan and Jarrett wouldn't have to duck to avoid hitting their heads. And that all their food, right down to their box of tea bags, wasn't stuck away up there, calling attention to how those wires were a defense against mice and pack rats.

Their canary, Billie, who'd been out of his cage and splashing in a small bath dish, got scared by the sight of strangers and flew up toward the rafters, scattering water and startling Ranger Logan into stepping backward without ducking. The back of his head sent the platform swinging, and Celia's box of watercolors slid off. Paint tubes rolled across the floor.

"I'll get them," she and Ranger Logan both said.

"Do you paint?" he asked, as Celia said, "They're just my paints."

Lizbeth served the pie while Celia poured coffee and Ranger Logan walked around looking at the watercolor pictures pinned up wherever there was wall space. Lizbeth thought they were the prettiest, warmest things in the cabin, even if they were just copies from magazines, and for Celia's sake, she was glad he was giving them attention.

"You painted these, Mrs. Whitcomb?" he asked. And when Celia nodded, he said, "They're very nice."

"Thank you," Celia said, neither her stiff voice nor her straight back unbending one little bit. As soon as everyone was sitting down, she went back to the subject of brush burning. Or, rather, to the reason she wanted it done.

"I have a hundred-sixty acres of land to protect," she said, ignoring Lizbeth's kick under the table. "Is the Forest Service going to take care of it for me?"

"We're doing the best we can to keep the fire danger down," Ranger Logan answered.

"But if a fire comes through, are you going to put it out for me?"

"I can't promise that."

"Or get the Forest Service to pay me for lost timber?"

Lizbeth saw Jarrett start to smile as though he thought Celia might be making a joke. Lizbeth knew better, and the ranger's answering voice was unyielding. "I'm sorry," he said, "but I can't let you do any burning. Not now. Not until the rains come this fall."

"And by then I won't need to!" Celia threw up her hands. "All right. I won't do any more brush burning right now. But if you think I'm going to let fire take out my timber, you've got another think coming!"

They sounded like brave words, but Lizbeth caught the glances the ranger and his brother exchanged. *Two women alone...*

"Look," Lizbeth said, "tell us what we can do. We can't lose this place."

"There's really not much," Ranger Logan said. "Clear trees away from the house..."

Celia interrupted him. "It's not the house I care about!"

"Be careful of cooking fires..."

She cut him off. "That's pap. I need real ideas. Would clearing firebreaks around our place help?"

"A firebreak around a hundred-sixty acres?" the ranger asked incredulously. "Mrs. Whitcomb, to cut a swath even a few feet wide—do you have any idea how much work that would be?"

"Lizbeth and I will do what we have to," Celia said, her voice snapping.

"Well, I can guarantee you can't do that," Ranger Logan snapped back.

Their arguing embarrassed Lizbeth, and she could see it was making the ranger's brother want to bolt. "Jarrett," she said, "would you like to see the rest of our place?"

———◆———

They returned to the corral, where Lizbeth whistled for Trenton and Philly to come and be admired. "They're sweet horses," Lizbeth said. "Though they're getting older, of course. One of these days I'd like to build them a proper barn to replace that open shelter they've got."

"Do you have neighbors to help?" Jarrett asked.

"I can build it myself."

"Including lifting the logs?"

"I know how to rig a pulley."

That made him grin. "Is there anything you and your aunt *can't* do?"

"Well, we *can't* agree on much," Lizbeth said, the words out of her mouth before she realized she was going to say them. She'd have stopped there, if it weren't for how Jarrett was waiting, as though he was really interested in hearing whatever she might say. "I mean," she continued, "Cel and I want different things. She wants to sell the timber off this place and get out, and I want to stay."

She turned to face him, letting her words tumble out. "I can't imagine anyplace in the world would be as nice as this is right here, and I'll die if I have to leave." She stopped short, mortified she'd paraded her feelings that way.

"I know what you mean," Jarrett said. "I wouldn't want to leave either, if this was my place."

———◆———

Later on, when Lizbeth was lying beside her aunt in the pole bed, listening to an owl and coyotes and knowing her aunt was awake, too, she said, "Cel, you could have been a little nicer. The ranger was just doing his job."

"Which he gets paid for doing."

"They were the first visitors we've had since that other ranger came through in the spring. I'd like to see them again."

"They weren't *visitors*, Lizbeth. You were forward to invite them inside."

"No, I was polite. Or have you forgotten what that means?"

"Don't be fresh," Celia said.

"You're the one that was fresh." Lizbeth turned her head away. "I bet they don't come back."

Washington State

◆

July 23, Afternoon

Seth peeled carrots while Abel poked among the slatted wooden crates lining the walls of the company cook tent. Cook himself had taken off after ordering them to prepare stew vegetables enough for fifty men. So there'd be no misunderstanding how many vegetables that was, Cook had stacked up the crates he wanted done. The two of potatoes, the one of onions. "And find the canned tomatoes, too," he'd said.

"You know," Abel told Seth, "there's other food here wouldn't take all this work."

They'd been pulling details together enough that they were getting to know each other's ways. Seth realized he did more than his share, but he was glad for how Abel put a gloss to things. Abel saw to it that their work—and the two of them—looked good, and for the first time, Seth was feeling and getting treated like the soldier he wanted to be.

Now, though, looking at the huge chore in front of them, Seth was impatient. "You gonna help?" he asked.

"Sure," Abel answered. "Here, I found the tomatoes

packed in with some pickles and stuff." He put an opened
crate atop the stacked crates. "Hey," he said, "hand me your
knife."

Seth watched him carefully slit under the flap of a box
marked with a skull and crossbones. "What's that?"

"Rat poison," Abel answered. "Folks ought to be careful
where they put this stuff." He tilted the opened box so
its powdered white contents sprinkled down through the
vegetables.

"What the hell are you doing?" Seth demanded. "You
want to kill somebody?"

"No, I'm taking care of us." Abel placed the rat poison box
in with the tomatoes. Then he pulled out a jar of pickles,
loosened the lid, and poured the juice on the box.

"By ruining all that food?" Seth said. "No washing will
make it safe now."

"The army won't miss a few vegetables," Abel said. He
poked at the box until the cardboard gave way and juice and
more white powder dripped down into the crates below.
"Leave it," he said. "I got to go tell Sarge we got us a
problem."

———◆———

Seth couldn't raise his gaze up, not when his only friend was
busy telling Sarge such barefaced lies. Seth was just waiting
for Sarge to bellow, *You expect me to believe that?*

Only, Sarge didn't. After asking a few suspicious questions,
he seemed to buy the whole story, right down to Abel's saying
the grocer who'd packed poison in the same container with
canned goods ought to make good on all the spoiled food.

"Cook didn't say to start anything else," Abel said, "but there's canned beans and bread enough for one meal. 'Course it's too soon to pull 'em out."

"Clean up here and haul this stuff off for burning," Sarge said. "Then I guess you two can take off." Only then did he throw Seth a troubled look. "Strange," he said.

———◆———

Seth told Abel, "That wasn't right."

"Nobody got hurt," Abel answered.

"How about the store man who's going to have to pay for that stuff?"

"The army won't track him down. Anyway, what do you care about someone you don't know?"

"What we did was wrong," Seth said.

"And making us peel vegetables when everybody else was off wasn't?" Abel demanded. "Let's go. I want to get to the baseball game in time to play some. Once people see my pitching arm, won't neither of us never have to work when there's a game on."

"I'm not that good a ballplayer," Seth said.

"They want me, they get you," Abel answered. "It's you and me, right? We're a team."

Cool Spring Ranger Station

◆

July 23, Night

Samuel finished the previous week's worth of notes. *Liars diaries*, the rangers called the reports they were supposed to keep up daily but rarely did. Since the reports were more often done in chunks of a week or two at a time, the facts had a way of getting mixed up. Also, everyone had heard the story about an honest ranger who once wrote that torrential rain kept him idle for a day. Supposedly the Forest Service had docked him the day's wages, with the result that ever since, a ranger with no other official business to report either "patrolled" or "maintained equipment."

Samuel considered what details to put in the current day's report. *Patrolled. Cleared trail. Warned folks about fire danger.* Same as most days. He knew that Jarrett, after just a week, was already chafing at the monotony of it.

A marauding bear had left the springhouse in need of reroofing, and he'd suggested Jarrett might tackle that job. Instead of welcoming the change, though, Jarrett had seemed to think the task was a demotion. The thought was clear on his face, though he'd set about the work without a word of protest.

That one keeps his own counsel, Samuel thought. *Maybe none of us Logans are good at saying what's on our minds.*

He put the report away and turned down the wick in the kerosene lamp. He was remembering the ride back to the station from the Whitcomb place. Jarrett had asked a dozen questions about homestead laws without once mentioning Lizbeth, but Samuel was sure that's who all the questions revolved around. "What did Mrs. Whitcomb mean about doing their six months and a day?" Jarrett had asked.

Samuel had explained that one of the requirements for proving up a homestead was living on it for more than six months a year. "Probably in the winter they stay in Wallace."

"It must be hard to keep up a place like that," Jarrett had said. "Two women alone, I mean. And lonely, too."

"I reckon." Samuel could have added, *Of course, men get lonely, too,* except there was no way he'd admit that to anyone.

Maybe that lonely side of ranger life was why he'd never quite got around to taking down that Wife Wanted poster. The rangers who put it up had meant it for a joke, but Hank Sickles, his best friend among them, had said, "Leave it for a while," and Samuel had.

Not that he really did want a wife. But the station sometimes seemed awful empty with just him by himself. Especially on evenings after he'd seen something extraordinary, like the time he'd watched a pair of half-grown, playful fawns snatch crab apples from their mother's mouth just to tease her. When you see a thing like that, you want to tell somebody.

Samuel had tried to sketch the scene into one of his notebooks, but although he could draw an apple that would pass scientific scrutiny, and do a passable deer, too, he didn't have the skill to put the story together right. That kind of drawing took talent like Mrs. Whitcomb's, though he couldn't see her painting deer, playful or otherwise.

He chuckled. Maybe he ought to be glad that poster hadn't brought results. What if he'd ended up with a wife as sharp-tongued as that one?

Distant thunder interrupted his musings. Boone came over to lean uneasily against Samuel's legs. "What do you think, boy?" Samuel said, rubbing behind the dog's ears. "Do we get along pretty well without a woman here?"

The next peal of thunder sounded closer, and the next one closer still. A bolt of lightning briefly turned the cabin bright as midday, and Boone tried to squeeze between Samuel's legs and the chair. Then a *craaack* many times louder was followed by the sounds of tearing wood and a tree crashing down through other trees.

"Jarrett?" Samuel called. "You awake?"

"Are you kidding?"

"We better go see if we've got us a fire to put out."

FIELD NOTES

The threat of dry lightning nags in the mind of a firefighter who guards acres of unburned fuel or struggles to bring control to land where trees already burn. He watches for clouds that might be forerunners of lightning storms. He frets over sullen weather that squats in a ragged gray heap on the southwestern horizon. He worries that a cold front is about to move in and bring him new problems.

Much of the year, over much of the earth, the thunderstorms that come with moving weather fronts carry enough rain to quench fires ignited by their lightning.

But sometimes, especially in a summer of drought, over parched land, thunderclouds form with only the barest amount of moisture. Enough moisture to put into motion the electrical imbalances that create lightning, but not enough moisture to make rain.

A fire must have heat to start. A bolt of lightning streaking down at temperatures hotter than the sun's surface brings far more than enough.

Placer Creek

July 23, Night

Jarrett's leg muscles ached and his lungs felt ready to explode as he fought to maintain the pace Samuel set. They went on foot, tools and knapsacks on their backs, hacking their way through trailless wilderness that horses couldn't negotiate. Tree branches swatted Jarrett's face and brambles scratched him as they climbed to a spot where they had glimpsed a small glow. Electricity in the close air made his skin tingle, and in the brightness of a lightning flash he saw the hair on his arms, below his rolled-up sleeves, stand up.

When they finally reached their destination, they found a meager fire lazily licking along the split trunk of a lodgepole pine. Half the tree angled down from the break to within arm's reach, and Jarrett hurried to it, assuming that's where they'd start.

"And what are you going to do if that other piece crashes down, and then a wind comes along and scatters flames everywhere?" Samuel asked.

Jarrett, not knowing what he was supposed to answer, remained silent.

"The first thing you do on a fire is figure out how you can get away from it if need be. Here, we're not far from a ridgeline that we could probably walk down. And in a pinch that clump of boulders we passed might make a decent shelter."

Samuel took off his knapsack before adding, "Running down the way we came would be tempting, but when a fire blows up, whatever you do, you don't want to get trapped in some gully."

He unstrapped his one-man saw and told Jarrett to pick up his ax. Then he pointed to a stand of skinny trees and shrubs that grew within the area where the burning pine might fall. "We'll down these first and drag them out of the way," he said. "Then dig a fireline and see what we've got."

Working in the poor light given off by the flickering flames, they chopped and sawed for an hour, clearing the area of wood and most other fuel. Then they worked another smoky hour to cut a foot-wide, bare-dirt line around what was left.

They smothered small spot fires inside the perimeter by breaking them up and spreading out the heat. The strategy wasn't too different from what Jarrett had figured out for himself, back on the Avery fire he'd tried to handle alone. Now, though, imitating Samuel's efficient moves, Jarrett gradually learned to make every shovel motion count. And after a while he was hardly wasting any muscle or wind at all on shallow scrapes and wild throws.

By that time the fire in the pine had about burned itself out.

Samuel straightened up, studied the scene, and nodded. "I think it's safe to go on. Ready for the next one?"

Jarrett, too exhausted to spend breath on words, just nodded.

"By the way," Samuel said, "you caught on fast, almost like you'd dug fireline before. Good work."

———◆———

They repeated the routine at the site of a second strike, this one in a lone snag that they reached just as the first light of dawn broke. Here, before they got started, Samuel pointed out a large patch of ground scorched in some previous fire. "That would be a place to escape to," he said. "Fire doesn't usually waste its time on old burns."

This time, while Jarrett cut fireline, Samuel brought down the snag itself, since it was spawning new blazes faster than they could put them out.

They worked furiously, and soon Jarrett was gulping for breath through the dry handkerchief Samuel had made him tie over his mouth and nose. Smoke hurt his eyes, and salty sweat stung his body. It stuck his clothes to him and made his hands and tool handles slippery.

Finally, though, Samuel said to stop—they had it.

Plodding back to the ranger station, Jarrett had all he could do just to keep upright.

As they went inside the wall phone sounded the two long rings that meant a call for Samuel rather than for someone else along the telephone line. Jarrett, dropping into the nearest chair, watched his brother close his eyes in weariness as he answered.

After listening a moment, Samuel said, "Sure. I'll get on it."

He put the earpiece into its hanger on the side of the tele-phone box. "Report of another smoke," he told Jarrett. "Probably one I can handle myself. Why don't you get some sleep?"

Sleep would feel so good, Jarrett thought. Then he got to his feet, because there was no way he would give up before his brother did. "It'll go faster with the two of us."

Homestead off Placer Creek

♦

July 24, Morning

Sunlight streamed down through the skylight, warming the batch of dough Celia was kneading.

Whenever did Lizbeth grow up enough to start thinking about boys? Celia wondered, as she lifted the far side of the dough and pulled it toward her and then leaned into it with the heels of her hands. *Or maybe she just wants a friend.* Celia spun the dough a quarter turn and lifted again. The question had been bothering her better than a week now, popping up when she least expected it.

She hoped her niece wouldn't fall for someone like Tom Whitcomb.

Not that all men had faults like Tom's. That Ranger Logan, for instance. He seemed bound to duty just as sure as Tom Whitcomb never even saw his. She'd wager Samuel Logan, however tired he might have been, had spent the night out meeting that electric storm head-on. Just as she and Lizbeth had walked their own place at dawn to be sure they had nothing burning.

Through the door open to the morning breeze, Celia could see Lizbeth replacing a broken rail at the corral. What kind of work was that for a young girl to be doing? And she never complained, except when Celia didn't let her take on even more.

Celia couldn't remember once in the last four years that Lizbeth had asked for a thing besides wire or nails or plant starts. Never once, until making that one comment last week about Jarrett Logan and his brother—"I bet they don't come back"—had Lizbeth let on that she missed other young people.

Celia kneaded the dough until it felt elastic with yeast coming to life. She covered it with a rucked towel and set it aside to rise. Then she walked out to where Lizbeth was working.

"I owe Dora Crane a letter," she said. "I was thinking that if I got to it one day soon, then we might drive it down to the mail drop. We could stop by the ranger station and leave a pie to make up for how ungracious I was to the ranger and Jarrett."

"If you want," Lizbeth answered, her voice stiff. Then she flung her arms around Celia so hard that Celia had to catch hold of a corral post to keep from being knocked off her feet. "Thank you!"

"Of course," Celia warned, "they might be away. Ranger Logan himself said this summer's keeping him busy."

FIELD NOTES

In the summer of 1910, rangers who were used to working in isolation suddenly found their forests filling with strangers.

With new fires breaking out daily through July and older ones stubbornly resisting control, the Forest Service's District One had no choice but to hire more and more men to fight them. By the end of the month, there were almost three thousand firefighters scattered across the district's several forests, one of which was the Coeur d'Alene.

District One Chief Forester W. B. Greeley would later say, "It was a case of hiring anyone we could get. We cleaned out Skid Road in Spokane and Butte. A lot of temporaries were bums and hoboes. In a bad fire year, the temporary is the weakest link in the chain."

He would also praise the help given by logging-camp crews and miners, just as Forest Service people would be quick to say good words about the efforts of homesteaders and townspeople, railroaders and others with a tie to the woods. But the truth was, the temporary firefighting force was a mixed and untrained lot.

Many of the men who went out to firelines had no experience with fires. Many spoke little English. Some were drifters who signed up under false names and lied about their hometowns. They went into the burning forests wearing the clothes they'd been recruited in, and the ones wearing street shoes or snug wool suits would regret that.

They worked for twenty-five cents an hour with board, thirty if they provided their own food. For some the regular work was a godsend. For more than a few, it was an invitation to devilment.

Placer Creek

July 24, Afternoon

Boone, brave again now that the lightning storm was over, accompanied Jarrett and Samuel when they set out for the smoke Samuel had been called to check on.

They had to climb halfway up a mountain to get to it, and Jarrett's aching legs felt more rubbery with every step. When they finally reached a smoldering log and small ground fire that seemed to be the source of the smoke, Samuel asked Jarrett what he thought they should do if the blaze got away.

Jarrett, cross and weary, snapped, "I don't know! You tell me!"

"And be to blame when what you don't know gets someone killed?"

"No! I've just had it with lessons for now," Jarrett said. Then, shamed by the disappointed expression on Samuel's face, he added, "Look, I want to learn all this stuff, but no more right now. Can't we just get done here?"

This last fire proved to be more stubborn than either of the ones they'd handled during the night, and they sawed and chopped and stooped over their shovels for several hours. The day's rising heat made the fire burn hotter, and it turned fighting the fire into miserable, broiling work. Jarrett got so thirsty he drank his last quart of water all in one wonderful moment, and then the liquid slogging around inside him, along with the sun beating down, made him want to vomit. And then he was desperately thirsty again long before Samuel declared, "That's enough. Let's pack up."

They were bushwhacking down the side of a steep slope, looking for a trail out, when something caught Boone's attention. His ears pricked forward, and his neck hair bristled.

"What's wrong, boy?" Samuel asked.

Boone whined softly and then dived down a game path that branched off at a sharp angle. He looked back once, saw Jarrett and Samuel were following, and went on.

Jarrett heard men's voices and then pleased-sounding, distinct words. "She ought to run up that face."

"Boone!" Samuel said softly, and the dog came instantly to his side.

"Jarrett, you stay here," Samuel ordered. "Boone, come."

Jarrett watched them make their way quietly toward the voices, and then, once they were out of sight, he waited impatiently to hear what was going on. Finally, when he couldn't stand the waiting anymore, he worked his way down to where he could see.

Directly below him, near a tree with a black scar, two men fanned a flame in a small pile of tinder. They were so intent on what they were doing that they didn't notice Samuel approaching until he was almost on them.

"Want to tell me what you're up to?" he said, a hand resting on the handle of his pistol. Boone, teeth bared, circled and growled.

"Nothing," the smaller of the two men mumbled, rising. "Honest. Making a cooking fire."

"Where's your food?"

The other man slowly got to his feet. "What if we said we ain't got none?" he asked. Only then did he raise his head to look directly at Samuel.

Jarrett saw recognition flicker across his brother's face. "Why aren't you on a fire crew? Didn't the Forest Service take you on?"

"I didn't like the job they offered," the man said. He waved a hand, and Jarrett noticed it was missing fingers. "They wanted to send me off on some fire that was to hell and gone."

"And so you decided to create a more convenient one?"

The smaller man said, "You got it wrong, Ranger. We was putting it out." He stamped on the tiny flames now licking from tinder into kindling. "Wasn't we, Tully?"

The one he'd called Tully ignored him. "What are you gonna do about it, Ranger?" Tully said. "Give me another Logan to get even with?"

"What I'm going to do," Samuel said, drawing his gun, "is haul you two before the sheriff in Wallace. You're under arrest."

"Not me," Tully said, turning his back on the pistol and starting away. Boone growled and looked to Samuel for direction.

Off to one side, on the uphill slope, the other man grabbed a rock and raised it to bring down on Samuel's head.

"Watch out!" Jarrett yelled, and he plunged down to help his brother. He saw the men below him look up, and he heard Samuel yell, "Jarrett, get back."

Then his foot caught on a tree root. He plummeted forward, and things got confused. There were shouts and sounds of running. Then Samuel was standing over him, whistling to Boone. "Let 'em go, boy."

◆

The walk back to the ranger station was strained.

"I'm sorry," Jarrett said. "I didn't mean to get in the way."

"I gave you an order," Samuel said. "I told you to stay where you were."

"The guy was going to hit you with a rock."

"Boone wouldn't have let him."

"You could have gone after them. You had your pistol, and Boone to help. And I would have helped."

Samuel didn't reply.

Jarrett thought for a moment. "I still don't get it. Why were they starting a fire on purpose?"

"My guess is they wanted to get hired to put it out," Samuel said. "They probably thought working a fire this close to Wallace would be easier than working one miles into the wilderness."

"But you knew who they were? You recognized the one."

"Tully. I met him once," Samuel answered. Then he added, "Of course, they might have had intentions other than making jobs for themselves. There's been talk of vagrants starting fires as cover for looting remote cabins."

Jarrett felt a chill. He could imagine men like those two doing that. Tully, with his missing fingers and vicious-sounding voice. The other man, smaller and cockeyed, more of a coward but ready to bring a rock down on Samuel's head.

◆

After supper the brothers sat on the ranger station porch cleaning soot from tools. Jarrett was still trying to make sense of the afternoon.

"Samuel, what did that one man, Tully, mean about having another Logan to get even with?" he asked.

"Just talk," Samuel answered. "He begrudges a run-in he had with Pop."

"What will you do about him?"

"Now that you've stopped me from arresting him and his friend for arson?" Samuel's cold voice told Jarrett he wasn't making a joke. "Not much besides seeing headquarters knows not to hire them on, and I doubt they'd apply there again anyway."

"You could tell the sheriff."

"I'll mention it, but he's got his hands full, too, this season. Most likely Tully and his friend will disappear into the crowds of strangers in town and in the woods, and they may or may not cause more mischief. My guess is they will."

A long silence followed as Jarrett considered the implications. Then he said, "Things would have gone different today if I wasn't your brother. You wouldn't have told a regular helper to stay where he'd be safe. And if you had and he'd done something as dumb as ignoring your orders and then

falling down that hill, you wouldn't have left those men alone
while you went to see to him."

Samuel shrugged. "I don't know that."

"Anyway," Jarrett said, "I've been thinking for a while now
I ought to get on a fire crew the way I set out to do. I'll put
that new roof on the springhouse like you asked, but then I'll
head on up to Wallace."

"You don't have to go. Just, if you stay around, obey my
orders."

"I really want to get out on a big fire anyway," Jarrett said.

"You'll have to obey orders anyplace you go."

"That's not the point," Jarrett said.

Samuel studied him. "No, it's not. You had it right before. I
did act differently today because you're my brother, and I
might again." He stood. "So maybe it's just as well you do go."

Jarrett searched his brother's face for some hint that
Samuel regretted how things had turned out, but if Samuel
had any feelings one way or the other, he was keeping them
to himself.

Part

TWO

Wallace

July 28, Morning

Jarrett entered Coeur d'Alene Forest headquarters in downtown Wallace behind two other men also seeking fire-fighting jobs. He got a quick impression of a house turned into an office, the fancy wallpaper above dark wood paneling now a place to hang notices and a calendar. He was surprised to see two women working at stations just inside the door, one at a typewriting machine. She glanced at Jarrett and the other newcomers and waved them farther inside. "You'll want to see Mr. Polson," she said.

Mr. Polson, in a suit and glasses, his hair neatly combed, sat at a scarred wooden desk.

One of the men who'd come in with Jarrett asked, "You still got work?"

A smile flitted across Mr. Polson's face. "Some. You know where we can hire an army?" The man responded with a blank look, and Mr. Polson sighed and picked up his pen. "Name?"

"Joe Sullivan." Sullivan nodded toward the other man. "That's Frank Naylor. We're together."

"Hometown?"

Sullivan shrugged. "All over."

"Vagrant," Mr. Polson said, and wrote it down.

Naylor said he didn't know what town to call home, since he'd been in the Montana State Prison so long.

The Forest Service man handed them slips of paper. "Take these to a hardware store, get yourselves each a shovel, and report back here for your orders. Pay's twenty-five cents..." He looked up hopefully. "Don't suppose either one of you is a cook?... No, I didn't think so. So, twenty-five cents an hour, and the government will pay for your transportation to fires and back here when you're discharged. You work at your own risk. No alcohol or disruptive behavior while on duty. Glad to have you. Next?"

Jarrett asked, "What do cooks get paid?"

"Whatever we can get them for," Mr. Polson answered, a smile again flickering across his face. "At four dollars or better a day, they're making more than I do. Why? Can you cook?"

"Not for an army. Twenty-five cents an hour will do fine, just so you send me somewhere I'm needed. I'm Jarrett Logan, from Avery."

Mr. Polson put down the pen and sat back in his chair. "Samuel's brother," he said. "I heard you were headed to the Cool Spring Station. He didn't have work for you there?"

"Not really. That is, he could use a hand, but patrolling and all's not really what I came for, and anyway—" Jarrett broke off awkwardly.

Mr. Polson gave him a questioning look but didn't pry. "Well," he said, "there's certainly fireline work if you want it.

Especially for fellows like you, showing up wearing decent boots and work clothes. Some men we've hired..." Mr. Polson's voice trailed off, and he shook his head. "Pitiful, really."

An inner door opened, and a man walked rapidly through, nodding without stopping on his way outside.

"That was Mr. Weigle," Mr. Polson volunteered. "My boss and yours, now."

And Samuel's, Jarrett thought. *Forest Supervisor Weigle, in charge of seeing the whole Coeur d'Alene doesn't burn up.* He'd heard Samuel say Weigle was doing his level best in a hard situation.

Mr. Polson logged Jarrett into the hiring book and wrote out a purchase order like he had given the others.

"Buy yourself a shovel, and if the hardware store's got them, you might pick up a couple of picks and mattocks. I'm going to send you up to the Graham Creek fire, which is growing enough they can probably use the extra tools." He wrote out another form. "If you hurry you can catch the train going that way. This will get you a ticket."

"I'm taking a train to a fire?" Jarrett asked.

"Beats walking."

Graham Creek

◆

July 29, Night

Jarrett arrived at the Graham Creek fire camp as everyone frantically rushed to control a blaze that had picked up and was threatening to jump a fireline. "Find a gap and pitch in!" someone yelled, running by.

Jarrett dropped his bedroll, grabbed his shovel, and headed toward the sounds of crackling fire, snapping branches, axes thudding into wood, and metal clanging against stone. His first sight of the crew was of fast-moving silhouettes working against pulsing curtains of crimson light.

Forcing himself not to shrink back from the fiery scene, he searched through the overwhelming confusion for someone who might say what exactly he was to do. The only person who even paused to glance his way just shouted, "Earn your pay!"

Jarrett struggled to grasp what was going on. This inferno was no more like the neat lightning strikes he'd worked with Samuel than a house fire was like a candle's glow.

The only thing that seemed the same was how the men striving to halt the belching onslaught stooped and stabbed, bent and dug. Jarrett moved into a space between two of the figures and smashed his shovel into a chunk of burning wood. He gathered up the pieces and flung them toward the flames, and then he stabbed at another piece of fire that he might throw back to the blaze. His shovel blade hit rock with a jolt that sent shock zinging up his arm. He caught his breath, waited out the wave of pain that quickly followed, and then he reached again for the same piece of fire and heaved it as far as he could throw.

Gradually, his work and that of the men around him began to pay off, as they protected and widened the threatened fireline, chopping off each groping finger of fire and throwing it back.

He'd never worked so hard or pushed his body so far. Breathing hurt deep in his lungs, and the shifting eddies of wind sent smoke swirling about his head, leaving him working blind for long moments.

He lost all feeling of time passing, until he began to wonder how much longer he could stand the hot aching in his shoulders or how his head felt like it was about to break open. Finally, the smoke blew away for a moment and Jarrett could see everything around him in light-edged clarity. He asked the nearest man, "How long do we go?"

"Until we get told to stop," the man answered. He appeared to be an older guy, stringy, lean. "Name's Elway," he said.

"Jarrett Logan."

They went back to work.

The order to knock off didn't come until the middle of the next morning, when their part of the fire finally seemed stalled where it was. Wearily trudging back to camp, Jarrett saw that Elway was even older than he'd first thought. The man's hair was gray under its coat of soot. Sweat running down Elway's face made it look like he'd painted himself with india ink.

With a start, Jarrett realized his own face must look the same way.

As they came into camp, they passed another crew heading out. "Poor sods," Elway said. "You think we had it bad, son, them's on day work has got it worse. Hotter than hell, and no hope of doing more than holding their own."

A woman—a fireguard's wife, Elway said—stood behind a table in an open-sided tent, ladling out stew and handing sourdough biscuits to all who wanted breakfast. Most did, but Jarrett felt too tired to stand up for another minute, much less hold a spoon and chew food.

"Anybody with sprains, burns, or cuts," the woman called, "I'll wrap ankles and put on ointment soon as I'm done here."

Jarrett decided that getting help for his blistered hands wasn't worth the effort of staying awake. Instead, he found a flat patch of ground a decent distance from the pack-mule string, spread out his bedroll, and lay down, expecting to fall asleep in an instant.

He hadn't counted on how being still would make him aware of the way his whole body hurt. Smoke and soot jammed his head, his throat was raw, and when he closed his eyes it felt like sandpaper scraping his eyeballs. He wondered if any of the other men were too tired to eat or ached as bad as he did. He wondered if any of them were asking themselves the same thing he was: How could he ever go back on that fireline and put in another night like the one he'd just had?

Homestead off Placer Creek
August 6, Evening

One chore and then another had kept Celia from writing Dora Crane, until Lizbeth was sure her aunt was putting off the trip to the mail drop and ranger station on purpose.

Confronted, Celia finally admitted, "I don't want it looking like you're chasing after that boy."

"Why would it look any more like that than like you're chasing after Ranger Logan?" Lizbeth asked, regretting the words the instant she'd said them. "I'm teasing, Cel," she added hastily. "The way you and the ranger disagreed, he couldn't misunderstand."

Still, it took a newspaper left by a passing logging camp foreman to jolt Celia into action. She read an account of the Pine Creek fires spreading and then took out a sheet of writing paper. "Perhaps tomorrow we can go to church, mail this, and stop by the ranger station," she said.

"Thank you!" Lizbeth exclaimed. Then she sobered. "Are you very worried about Mrs. Crane?"

Celia answered, "I'm not worried so much as I'd just like to hear she's all right."

Lizbeth pictured the large motherly woman who had befriended them during their first winter in Wallace. Between Dora Crane and old Mrs. Marston, they'd quickly been made welcome.

Mrs. Marston, who owned a boardinghouse, had given them a room and meals in exchange for help with the cooking, an arrangement they'd returned to each winter since.

Dora Crane, in Wallace with her own children for the school year, had introduced Celia to shopkeepers and Lizbeth to teachers.

Lizbeth and Celia had missed Dora Crane ever since several Pine Creek families put up a schoolhouse so they could stay on their places year-round.

Lizbeth hoped Mrs. Crane and her big family were all right.

———◆———

While Celia wrote the letter, Lizbeth made a mincemeat pie. She wasn't nearly as good a baker as her aunt, but she gave it her best effort.

She hoped the ranger and his brother wouldn't be away on patrol. Surely, Lizbeth thought, the Forest Service gave Sundays off.

She tested the oven's heat with her elbow and then put the pie in. While it was baking she scanned the fire stories scattered across the newspaper's eight pages, looking for any fires close enough they might be a threat to her and Celia. She wondered if Jarrett Logan had got involved in fighting any of them.

She'd liked how he'd understood her feelings about this

place. How he hadn't laughed at her wish to make a go of things or her ideas for how it could be done.

With a sigh, Lizbeth turned back to the newspaper's front page and began reading it more carefully. For once she was seeing a paper that was current—out just Thursday, and here it was only two days later. Most of the time, living so isolated, she didn't know what was going on elsewhere until after it was long done and over.

Graham Creek

August 7, Morning

On Graham Creek, Jarrett was partway through another shift of cutting fireline.

One of the first things he had learned on his new job was that night and early morning were make-progress time on a wildfire. The still air, higher humidity, and cooler temperatures let firefighters go on the offensive.

For almost a week now, he'd been part of a day crew steadily carving an ever longer trench designed to starve the advancing fire of fuel. At first he hadn't been able to see beyond his own job. Then, as he'd been put on one task and then another, he'd started to understand how the various jobs fit together.

This was his first time as an axman, pushing the fireline into new territory by chopping down brush and small trees.

Not far behind, sawyers using crosscut saws took down the bigger stuff, cutting through downed logs and dropping trees with branches that hung over the fireline's path.

A third group followed them, raking away all the small, burnable fuel—pine duff and sticks, leaves and grass—and scraping the line down to bare soil.

And word was, when conditions were right, a low blaze would be run along the inside of the break to widen it with a charred black line.

It was all backbreaking, arm-numbing work, but Jarrett had built up calluses and lung power, and that helped. And the crews were working far enough in front of the main fire that its heat didn't blast them the way it did when they had to dig hot line, laboring close to the flames.

Of course, working so far ahead of the spreading fire also meant they had to cut a longer trench than they would have closer in, and Jarrett had asked Elway the sense in that.

"Buys time," Elway had answered. "What you want is to strike a line just big enough so you can get it done before the fire can outflank you."

"Sounds reasonable."

"Just theory," Elway had said. "Me, I'd put money on the losing side of a fixed fight before I'd bet on outguessing a fire."

Now the foreman called, "Take ten!"

Jarrett leaned his ax against some saplings he was cutting down and sank gratefully to the ground. Up and down the line, men guzzled water, tamped tobacco into pipes, and swatted at the plaguing wasps.

The routine had become so familiar, Jarrett found it hard to believe he'd ever done anything else. Or that he had ever been as raw as he was his first night out here.

Remembering, Jarrett smiled. It seemed like a lifetime ago.

Elway, resting nearby, asked, "You thinking of a good joke?" The two of them had partnered up, and they were getting a name for being a reliable team.

"I guess, with me the butt of it. Elway, you think we're doing any good? We're working our hearts out, but from what I hear, this fire just keeps jumping in new directions. I think it's bigger than ever."

Elway shrugged. "At least we're still in the battle. The thing to be scared of is a fire you can't fight."

"You think this one could get like that?"

"Yeah," the old man said. "Enough things go wrong, any fire can."

Cool Spring Ranger Station

August 7, Afternoon

"I'm really not sure this is appropriate," Celia said when they finally pulled up at the hitching post in front of the ranger station. She surveyed the neat cabin and outbuildings without making any effort to climb down from the wagon.

"Aren't we going in?" Lizbeth asked. "We can't just leave the pie on the porch and take off."

"I was just thinking—it seems hard to believe this place and ours have been cut from the same woods."

Impatience and frustration warred in Lizbeth. "That's what I've been telling you, Cel. We could make something of our place, too, if you'd just give us a chance."

"No. This place doesn't have to make money. Ours does. Well, are you coming?"

Celia, Lizbeth by her side, knocked on the cabin's closed door. Then she stepped back, apparently just then noticing the poster that said Wife Wanted.

"Oh, lord," Celia said. "I knew this was a mistake. What kind of man . . . Lizbeth, let's go."

Samuel Logan and his dog came around the side of the

house. Boone ran up and greeted them like people the ranger had already cleared, while the ranger himself showed surprise and pleasure and then concern. "Mrs. Whitcomb— Lizbeth—are you all right? Is there a problem up your way?"

"No," Celia answered stiffly. "Not at all. We had things to do in town and just thought to stop by..."

"To give you this," Lizbeth said, holding out the mince-meat pie. "It's not as good as the pies that Celia makes, but it was her idea. It's to say we're sorry you didn't get a more polite welcome at our place."

"That's enough, Lizbeth," her aunt said. "Ranger Logan, we'll just leave it and be on our way."

The ranger nodded, appearing relieved. "Thank you. It looks delicious," he said. He started to take it but then drew back his grease-coated hands. "Shop work," he said. "Would you mind setting the pie inside? I'd say to put it down out here, but even Boone's got his limits."

Lizbeth opened the door and went in, leaving her aunt standing red faced in front of the Wife Wanted poster. *She's probably wondering if he thinks she's come to apply,* Lizbeth thought. *Serves her right.*

She heard Ranger Logan, his voice muffled, say, "Some friends put it up. The poster, I mean. As a gag."

"I assumed so," Celia answered. "I'm surprised your employer doesn't require you to remove it."

Lizbeth had hoped she'd find Jarrett inside, but it didn't sound as though anyone was there. "Ranger Logan?" she called. "I was just wondering, is your brother...?"

"Jarrett's on the Graham Creek fire," he answered. "He left a little over a week ago."

"Oh, I see," Lizbeth said, trying not to sound disappointed.

She carried the pie to a table, where she moved aside a pile of scrapbooks. A dried leaf fell from between them, and she put it back. Then, curious, she opened the top book. The page she turned to held a pressed stalk of Indian paintbrush neatly labeled with its Latin name and the date and place it had been picked. A meticulously detailed sketch on the facing page showed the plant it had come from.

Outside, Celia was saying that they really had to be going. That they had their hands full with all the work on their place.

"Oh?" the ranger asked. "Have you been cutting that firebreak you talked about?"

Glancing through the open doorway, Lizbeth saw Celia press her lips tight before answering, "Some."

The truth was, in several days of dawn-to-dark work, they'd made so little progress even Celia had conceded the project was hopeless.

Trying to put down her disappointment over Jarrett's absence, Lizbeth turned another page in the scrapbook and then another, idly at first and then with increasing interest. Finally, she carefully carried the book outside. "I hope you don't mind, Ranger Logan, but I saw this when I was clearing space for the pie and I wanted to show my aunt."

Celia glanced down quickly before looking more closely at an inked drawing beside a faded blue spray of lupine. As Lizbeth had, she turned to another page and then another. She asked the ranger, "Is this your work? The illustrations are so..." She seemed to search for a word. *"Exact."*

"They help me fix details in my mind," he said almost apologetically.

"Are the other scrapbooks full of flowers, too?" Lizbeth asked.

"No, they're different things," he answered, reaching for the one Celia held and then again withdrawing his hands when he saw the grease.

"Why don't I put it inside?" Celia said. "If I may, I'd like to see the others."

Lizbeth studied her aunt and the forest ranger as they sat at the table with his scrapbooks open around them. One book held leaves and needle clusters from trees, with sketches of bark so carefully drawn that a person could almost feel how rough it would be. Two others contained just drawings and notes, one book devoted to insects and one to animal tracks and homes.

"These must have taken years to put together," Celia said. "I can't imagine... What got you started?"

"Just passing winter evenings, after it turned out I had no skill for taxidermy and didn't care for braiding horsehair," the ranger answered. "But then the books turned out to be a good way for me to learn some of the things new rangers are coming out of school knowing."

"These collections are lovely," Celia said. "Worth treasuring."

"I reckon they're the one thing I own that I care about,"

Ranger Logan told her. "I just wish…" The telephone rang two long rings, and he didn't finish his sentence.

Going over, he picked up the earpiece and leaned close to the speaking funnel. "Cool Spring Station," he said. "Ranger Logan here."

He listened a moment and then asked, "How bad?" Then he said, "I've got a few shovels and one double-bit ax I can spare. You want me to pack them in, as long as I'm going?… Okay then, I'll get started first thing tomorrow and count on you guys to keep an eye on things out this way."

Hanging up, he turned back to Lizbeth and her aunt. "The Pine Creek fire has broken loose again," he said. "I swear that fire's got more lives than a barnyard cat."

"I just mailed a letter to a friend in Pine Creek," Celia said. "I hope she's all right."

"Most folks out that way have been fortunate so far," he said. "Tell me her name, and I'll keep an ear out for it."

"Crane," Celia told him. "Dora Crane. Her husband is Nathaniel Crane."

"I'll remember," the ranger said. "And now, I hate to run you all off, but…"

"But you've got a lot of getting ready to do," Celia finished for him. "Thank you for your hospitality and for letting us see your scrapbooks."

◆

They said their good-byes, and then Celia leaned down from the wagon. "Ranger Logan," she said, "Lizbeth and I will be attending a church picnic in the town park next Sunday. We could pack some extra food, if you would care to be our guest. Jarrett, also, if he's back."

Ranger Logan appeared as surprised as Lizbeth was. But after a moment's hesitation, he said, "Why, I'd like that. With this fire season as bad as it is, I don't know just where I'll be that day, but if I can make it into Wallace, I will. And if Jarrett returns here once he's done at Graham Creek, I'll pass on the invitation."

"*If?*" Lizbeth asked. "Doesn't he live with you?"

"Oh no," the ranger answered. "At least, I don't think so."

Driving away, Lizbeth said, "Cel, how could he not know if Jarrett lives with him?"

Celia shook her head. "I've no idea. No idea at all."

Wallace

✦

August 8, Morning

Mr. Polson of the Coeur d'Alene Forest headquarters office stuck a colored pin in the wall map. These days the fire picture changed faster than he could add pins to show what was burning and where the rangers had their crews.

Most fire seasons settled into a rhythm men could work around, with fires blazing up and dying down along with the weather. The crews could take it easy some, between the worst bursts of work. And maybe once in a while, they could stay on a fire long enough to put it all the way out.

This year, though, with things so dry, the lulls weren't happening. No one was getting any rest. And as for a crew being able to put a fire out altogether...

This year a fire boss just hoped to get a good enough perimeter around a fire that it could be left to burn. A few men might be spared to patrol the surrounding trench, but the main crew would have to go on to the next fire.

Sighing, Mr. Polson turned to the paperwork stacked on his desk. More problems, all of it. Where was he supposed to scrape for new firefighters when there wasn't anybody left to hire? President Taft had authorized the use of military troops, but Mr. Polson wouldn't count on that help until he saw the soldiers.

And he needed to find a cook for that camp that was losing people over canned tomatoes served three meals a day.

Also, he should ask store owners to search their backrooms for overlooked tools. New shovels had gotten rare as a January thaw.

What a way to spend a fire season!

He'd like to be out on the firelines himself instead of tied down here. Young again and eager, like that Logan boy he'd sent to Graham Creek. He hoped the kid was doing all right. Samuel Logan had been in asking about him.

That was the day Samuel had spotted a pair of arsonists coming out of a town bar. They'd got away from him once, but this time they spent a night in jail before a judge turned them loose.

As for Samuel, he'd sounded relieved to hear Jarrett was working under Will Morris, a ranger who knew what he was doing. "Not that Jarrett can't take care of himself," Samuel had said, "but I'd hate to see him on some crew where the boss didn't know up slope from down."

"I'm afraid there are some," Mr. Polson had said. "But your brother seems like a young man with his head on his shoulders."

"He's got some learning to do," Samuel had replied, "but I think you're right."

Washington State

◆

August 9, Morning

Seth, straightening to rest his back, wondered why the officers were busying about so much. They hurried from tent to tent, and huddled over papers, and put their heads together with the sergeants'.

He wished one of those sergeants would think to send him some help. This was his second day at pickaxing and digging a new latrine ditch, and his back and shoulders throbbed.

Seth had been getting jobs like this ever since Abel played that rat-poison trick to get him and Seth off kitchen duty. Sometimes Seth wondered if Sarge had guessed what was done and was punishing him.

Other times Seth wondered if Sarge was just trying to find a job Seth would refuse.

Well, Seth wouldn't refuse any—even if he could have without winding up in a guardhouse.

Abel said Seth was being a sucker. For some reason Abel never got the same kind of attention from Sarge. *Harassment*, Abel called it, when, night after night, he urged Seth to ease up. "Why you work so hard, Brown?" he'd ask. "Where's the percentage?"

Finally Seth had asked him, "What do you care, anyway?"

"I care about you, buddy," Abel had answered. "Someone got to."

Now Abel came over to the ditch and looked down. "You just as well stop digging," he said. "Rumor is we're moving out."

"Where to?" Seth asked.

"Idaho, to put out forest fires. Heard it early this morning."

Seth flung down his shovel. Sarge piling on needed work was one thing, but leaving Seth to sweat over a job there wasn't no point to was another. "So I done all this for nothing?"

Abel said, "Looks like it. Maybe Sarge needs a lesson taught him."

"What do you mean?"

"Nothing special. Just a thought 'bout how good getting even can feel. Say, after supper, you want to celebrate our last night in camp? I can work a deal to get us passes."

"Yeah," Seth said, still fuming. "Why not?"

They found most of the company gathered at a saloon bar, although Sarge and his cronies were missing. Seth would have hung back, but Abel pulled him into the group.

One of the men said, "You hear Sarge hurt his ankle bad? Oddest thing, a hole opening up when he stepped into his tent. Gophers, he figured."

In his mind Seth heard the words *How good getting even can feel.* But it had to be coincidence—or was it? He glanced at Abel, but his friend was looking as surprised and interested as anybody.

The bartender came over, and Seth ordered a beer.

A guy Seth didn't know well said, "Hey, Junior, you old enough for that?"

A man from Seth's squad answered, "'Course he is. He's ours, ain't he? Part of the fighting Twenty-fifth."

While soldiers joked and hoisted glasses, Abel stepped close and said, quiet enough for just Seth to hear, "We're the real team, Brown, you and me."

Later, walking back to camp, Seth asked, "Abel, you didn't have nothing to do with what happened to Sarge, did you?"

"Of course not, buddy," Abel answered. "I wouldn't do nothing you didn't want."

Homestead off Placer Creek

August 13, Afternoon

It was another Saturday, and Lizbeth was arguing with Celia again.

"You invited them to a picnic," Lizbeth said. "What are Samuel and Jarrett going to think, if they show up and we're not there?"

"Ranger Logan," Celia corrected. "They would think we're showing good judgment, staying home to look after our place. Besides, with the fires so much worse, the Logans are probably off fighting them."

"You don't know the fires are worse."

"Use your nose, Lizbeth. You think the smoke's not increasing by the day?"

Lizbeth turned away. She knew her aunt was right, but she hated to admit the increased fire danger when there wasn't any way to know just how bad *worse* was. Or from just how far away—or how near—the smoke came. The wind had picked up a couple of days earlier, blowing in veering, fitful gusts, and then a new layer of hazy, rich smoke had settled in.

"Look, Cel," she said, "why don't you let me go into town

long enough to get some news? I can ride Trenton in tomorrow in time for the picnic, spend the night with Mrs. Marston, and then Monday, before coming back here, I'll go to the Forest Service office and ask what's going on. Cel, please?"

"I don't like you riding that far by yourself."

"You've done it."

"Not when the woods were crawling with who knows what riffraff."

"I don't know what riffraff you're talking about. Most of the firefighters we've seen have been men who live here, same as us," Lizbeth said.

Her aunt stared out to where veiling smoke had turned the hills into looming, indistinct shapes. "I *would* like to know if Dora Crane has written."

"I'll stop at the mail drop," Lizbeth promised. "And I'll bring back a newspaper, too."

❖

When bedtime came without Celia having said a definite *no*, Lizbeth knew she'd won. Maybe by this time two nights from now, they'd know the fire situation wasn't nearly as bad as they feared. Maybe when she left their gulch, she'd walk out of smoke into clear air. Then, in Wallace, she could enjoy the picnic and not worry.

She wondered what her chances were of seeing Jarrett. She wondered at herself, wanting to see him so much, when they'd only met that one day.

She'd thought maybe her aunt was just a bit interested in Ranger Logan, too, since the picnic invitation was her idea, but Celia had hardly mentioned him since giving it.

"Cel," Lizbeth whispered, "are you awake? Are you sure you don't want to go into Wallace with me?"

Celia didn't answer, but her breathing was so absolutely soundless she had to be pretending sleep.

Lizbeth turned over and then over again. Sometimes this bed was impossible to get comfortable in.

"Lizbeth, will you stop thrashing about!" Celia exclaimed. She threw the covers back and stood up. "No, I do not want to go to Wallace. Do you want a cup of tea? I must say, I do not like things this unsettled."

Graham Creek

◆

August 14, Morning

Jarrett, who had returned to working night shifts, came awake confused by sudden commotion. The clay-colored sun was still on the morning side of the smoke-filled sky, so he hadn't been asleep more than a couple of hours. A pair of exhausted-looking men that Jarrett didn't recognize sank to the ground near him. Someone thrust cups of coffee into their hands.

Beyond them the crew boss bent over a man lashed to a makeshift stretcher. Jarrett could hear the crew boss say, "Take it easy, now. We'll get you on a train and to a hospital in no time."

One of the newcomers muttered, "Thank god."

"What happened?" Jarrett asked.

"Don't know exactly," the man answered. "We were putting out a spot fire when Benny—that's Benny that's hurt—brought his ax down on his foot and fell into the flames. Why he did it..."

The other newcomer, swaying with fatigue, said, "I can tell you. Benny was too wore-out to be careful like he ought.

We pulled him out fast as we could and were pure lucky we didn't kill ourselves doing it."

The crew boss came over and asked, "Does your outfit know about the accident?"

"No," one of the men answered. "We were closer to here than to our camp."

"Well, once you get some rest, you better get word down. Meanwhile, I'll have a couple of my fellows take your friend into Wallace." He looked around. "Volunteers?" His gaze rested on Jarrett's friend, Elway. "How about it?" he said. "You know as much as anyone about caring for injuries."

Elway nodded. "Sure, we'll go," he said. "Logan here, and me." He turned to Jarrett. "That is, if you're willing?"

"Sure," Jarrett said. "Why not?"

"Thanks, then," the crew boss said. "And you better check in at headquarters before returning. They may want to send you on someplace else."

Jarrett rolled up his blanket, wrinkling his nose at a new, scorched, sweet stink that underlay the smoke. It reminded him of burned hair and meat dropped into a fire. And of how a boot smells when you get it too close to a campfire.

"Smells like the fires trapped some animals," he said. Elway shot him a quick look, and one of the newcomers snorted.

No, not the man, Jarrett thought. But as soon as he thought it, he knew it was so.

Fearfully, and unable to stop himself, Jarrett went over to look.

Benny was a white man. Jarrett could tell that from some

of the skin showing where his shirt had been torn away. But
Benny's face—under its coat of soot, one side was bright red
and blistered. And his chest was burned black as the base of a
pine tree hit by fire time and again. That was the worst of
him, worse than how his leg was swollen around the top of
the boot that the crew boss was carefully cutting away.

But not much worse than the soft keening coming from
someplace deep inside him as he drifted in and out of consciousness.

Elway came up, and Jarrett heard him catch his breath.
"God," he said. "I wasn't expecting...Jarrett, I'm sorry."

"Elway," the crew boss said, "you want to give me a hand
cleaning out this ax cut?"

Jarrett slipped off behind some bushes, where he vomited
until it felt like his whole insides might rip out. Then he got
water and rinsed his mouth and washed his hands.

And then he went back to Elway and the crew boss and
Benny. "What can I do to help?" he asked.

◆

With the injured man on a pole-and-blanket stretcher suspended between the back end of one mule and the front of
another, Jarrett and Elway headed down the mountain to the
tiny Graham Creek train station. A man detailed to return
the animals to camp walked at the lead mule's head, while
the two of them walked beside Benny, trying to protect him
from branches and bad jolts.

Long before the walk ended, Benny lost consciousness
again, which seemed a blessing. And they reached the station
just as one of the infrequent trains pulled in. A conductor

helped them turn the stretcher blankets into a pallet at one end of the passenger car, and they settled back for the trip to Wallace.

Almost at once Jarrett began trembling, and cold shakes racked his whole body.

Elway pulled a whiskey flask from a pocket and held it out. "This will make you feel some better," he said. "Just go real easy. Benny's going to need us both."

———◆———

Sometime later, after they'd stanched fresh bleeding from Benny's foot and again changed the cloths covering his burns, Jarrett asked, "Elway, is he going to live?"

"Maybe," Elway said. "There's not that much of him burned, bad as he looks, and the wound's not deep as it could have been."

"But his face won't ever look right, will it?"

"No. And I don't know how much eyesight he'll have."

———◆———

A lot later, watching Benny's chest go up and down, which seemed a miracle in itself, Jarrett said, "I didn't imagine this, when I set out to fight fires."

"Course not," Elway said. "Anyway, why did you set out?"

"Lots of reasons. The most immediate one being I got fired from the railroad." Jarrett went on to tell about the disaster of his one day working as a spotter.

Elway chuckled. "Sounds like my first job," he said. "I'd just started sheep tending when I saw a coyote make off with a lamb. Tracked it all the way to its den and got rid of it and its pups, and then came back and found my two hundred ewes and lambs scattered halfway to creation. I got fired, too. Part of growing up, I guess.

"Hey," he said. "It just dawned on me, we got us a night or two in Wallace. Not exactly the biggest place, but..."

He eyed Jarrett uncertainly. "Though, maybe instead of carousing around, you'll want to look up your brother."

"I should," Jarrett said. "I owe him an apology for acting like I knew a lot more than I did."

"And weren't you telling me something about a young lady?"

"Lizbeth. I doubt I'll get to see her. She and her aunt live on a homestead pretty far out."

"They may be in town," Elway said. "It wouldn't surprise me if a number of homestead families didn't evacuate the backcountry till the fire danger's past."

"You don't know Lizbeth and her aunt."

"And you know 'em pretty well?"

"No. I just met them once, but Lizbeth told me all about how things are with them. She got me thinking about how different people want different things from this country."

Elway shook his head. "Girls do that, talk everything to death and then expect you to think about what they said. That's the reason I ain't never married. All that thinking females require makes my head ache."

They shared a quiet laugh at that, and then Benny groaned and their laughter drained away. Elway opened a canteen and dribbled a little water in Benny's mouth. "I don't want him to choke," Elway said, "but he's got to be thirsty."

Jarrett said, "I keep wondering if Benny would be alive if I'd been the one with him when he fell in that fire. I don't know if I would have gone in after him. And even if I had, I don't know if I'd have figured how to bring him out of the woods the way those men did."

"I think you would have," Elway said. "Look how you've handled all you had to today. You've seen what was needed and done it, and can't nobody do more than that."

———◆———

The Wallace stationmaster called for an ambulance, and Elway and Jarrett helped a hospital attendant transfer Benny to the horse-drawn conveyance. "No need for you to ride along," the attendant said. "Looks like you got him here as good as could be expected."

"That's it?" Jarrett asked Elway once the ambulance had driven away. "What do we do next? Let headquarters know he's here?"

"I reckon," Elway said. "And then I'm planning to look me up some folks and put in a night to remember." Again he eyed Jarrett uncertainly. "You're welcome to come along…"

"Thanks anyway," Jarrett said. "I can keep busy. And I'll make the headquarters report. I'll say you'll stop by tomorrow."

"Not too early tomorrow!" Elway said.

"Not too early," Jarrett agreed.

Wallace

◆

August 14, Night

The downtown stores were dark except for two-storied buildings where people lived in upstairs rooms. An electric light shone in the Forest Service office, though. Inside, Jarrett found a dispatcher working the telephone switchboard and Mr. Polson going through papers at his desk.

Jarrett made his report, doing his best to answer Mr. Polson's concerns. "Elway, the guy I was with, thinks Benny will be all right."

"I hope so," Mr. Polson said. "I'm afraid that if this fire season doesn't end soon, we're going to see more and more men hurt because they're too tired to take care of themselves." He rubbed his face. "And you? You ready to go out again?"

"Any time," Jarrett answered, though it was a lie. He just knew he'd go, whether he was ready or not. "But I'd like to wait and go with Elway, if that would be okay. He'll be coming by tomorrow, and we've kind of partnered up."

"That's Elway Jorgenson?" Mr. Polson asked. He chuckled. "A good firefighter," he said. "And a hard drinker. Well, we'll

see. Why don't you check in here around midmorning?" He
started to return to his paperwork but then looked up again
when Jarrett didn't leave. "Anything else?"

"I was just thinking that if you could give me till noon or
so, I'd have time to hike down to the Cool Spring Station and
see my brother."

"Samuel's not there," Mr. Polson said. "We've been sending him straight from one job to another, and the current
one's likely to keep him away for a couple more days. You can
leave a message here for him, if you want. Which reminds
me..." He pulled papers off a spindle until he got down to a
folded sheet with Jarrett's name on it. "He left one for you."

Jarrett read, *Mrs. Whitcomb and her niece asked us to a church
picnic in the town park Sunday, August 14. I doubt I'll make it, but
if you want, go on.*

That was today, Jarrett thought. He'd missed it by just
hours.

Mr. Polson, who apparently knew what was in the note,
looked sympathetic. "It probably got canceled, anyway," he
said. "With so many of Wallace's men out fighting the hill
fires, not much social's been going on."

———◆———

Jarrett, once he was outside, considered where to go next. Mr.
Polson hadn't mentioned putting him up for the night, and it
was too late to hike to the ranger station—and no reason to
go there anyway, with Samuel away.

Probably Mr. Polson had expected Jarrett would get a bed
in a Wallace hotel, but Jarrett hadn't been paid yet for his
Graham Creek work and didn't have money for more than a

day or two's food. He ended up wandering until he reached
the town park, where he spread his bedroll under a tree and
stretched out. If the deserted park held any hint of an earlier
picnic, he didn't see it.

He was almost asleep when it occurred to him that if Lizbeth and Celia had come to town, they might have chosen to
sleep over rather than drive back to their place at night. Probably they'd stay at that boardinghouse Lizbeth had mentioned, in one of the steep hillside neighborhoods directly
above the downtown's southern edge. He wished he knew an
address or at least which street it was on.

Maybe, come morning, he'd just go walk around up there,
on the off chance....

———————◆———————

He woke up at dawn to the sounds of many feet passing
by, and the creaks of freight wagons, and shouted orders. A
sheriff's deputy was looking down at him. "Gonna have to
ask you to move, son," he said. "The army's taking over the
park."

Wallace

◆

August 15, Morning

As Lizbeth walked to the Forest Service office, she heard fire stories being told all around her. People talked about narrow escapes and burned timber. About how Wallace was threatened or how it wasn't. Of how, if Wallace was to burn, the fire would probably come from Placer Creek. Or it wouldn't.

Some said that things would be okay now that the soldiers had come to help. Others maintained that two companies of men was a spit in the bucket, and who was the government trying to fool?

Across the street from Lizbeth, blackened tatters of fabric flapped above a store window. An ash-coated stick fell from the sky and landed at her feet. Probably one like it, only still glowing from whatever forest fire it had floated in from, had turned the store's awning to burned ribbons.

Periodically, loud booms reverberated from nearby hills, and men close by her were arguing about whether the city was wasting its money paying for the blasting. "Dynamite ain't gonna shake rain loose where there ain't no clouds to shake it from," one said.

"The dynamiter gave his guarantee," another argued. "Anyway, you got a better idea?"

Lizbeth bit her lips. She, for one, didn't, although she thought the whole idea of exploding rain was silly.

She was about to enter the Forest Service office when she heard her name called. Spinning around, she saw Jarrett.

"What are you doing here?" she asked. "I looked for you yesterday. The picnic got canceled, but Mrs. Marston—that's my landlady at the boardinghouse where Cel and I stay in the winter—said I might invite you back there."

"I didn't get in until late last evening," Jarrett said. "Look, I've got to check in here, but then..."

———◆———

Inside, there was enough going on that no one had time for them for several minutes. Then, finally, a man that Jarrett introduced as Mr. Polson came over. "So," he said to Jarrett, with a quick smile, "you found her."

Lizbeth darted a glance Jarrett's way. *So he was looking for me, too!*

"You can take the rest of today off," Mr. Polson told Jarrett, "but be back here first thing in the morning. I'm going to send you down to the St. Joe with some equipment we're getting repaired."

"I'm not going back on a fireline?" Jarrett asked.

"Oh, there's enough burning down there—they'll need you one place or another. I wouldn't be sending you out by yourself except we're so shorthanded, and Elway told me you can find your way through a forest good as anybody."

"Elway was here already?" Jarrett asked. Lizbeth thought he sounded surprised.

"I tracked him down," Mr. Polson answered. "We had a crew put together but no one to guide it, so I sent him along."

"Elway and I were kind of a team."

"So he said," Mr. Polson replied. "He said to tell you good luck and to remember what he told you. Guess you know what it was?" When Jarrett didn't offer an explanation, he continued, "Well, I guess that's that. You've got until tomorrow morning, seven A.M., to report back here." He nodded at Lizbeth—"Nice to meet you, young lady"—and started to turn away.

"Excuse me," Lizbeth said, "but I'd like to know about the fire situation in the Placer Creek area. My aunt and I have a homestead up one of the smaller gulches."

"I don't know what to tell you," Mr. Polson said. "Several fires are burning in there, but at the moment we've got the upper hand on most. And one of those companies of soldiers that just got here is likely to be sent in to help."

"Where are the rest of the soldiers going?" Jarrett asked.

"Probably Avery. The situation down there is getting more serious by the day." Mr. Polson paused. "Didn't you say that's your home?"

"My father lives there," Jarrett answered, "but I don't, anymore."

———◆———

"That's something I meant to ask you about," Lizbeth said, once they were outside again. "Just where *do* you live?"

"Wherever the Forest Service sends me," Jarrett said.

"And when the fire season is over?"

"I don't know. Right now, it doesn't feel like it ever will be." He kicked a rock so hard it spun across the street. "Once, *just once*, I'd like to see a fire stopped in its tracks." He broke off. "You don't need to hear that. What have you been doing?"

"Besides worrying about fires?" she asked.

They wandered slowly, turning down one side street and then another. She told him about visiting the ranger station and about how Samuel and her aunt had gotten along so well. "It was your brother's scrapbooks that did it," Lizbeth said. "All those lovely drawings, and Cel..."

Lizbeth realized Jarrett wasn't listening. His attention had focused on a trio of men slouching in the open doorway of a warehouse. When one of them turned and looked toward them, Lizbeth felt Jarrett tense. He took her elbow and said, "Let's go another way."

Wallace

August 15, Afternoon

"You got two hours," Sarge told Seth and Abel. "Get going."

Their outfit had pulled into Wallace about 5 A.M., after spending the better part of three days and nights riding trains. They'd marched to a park, made camp there, and now the men were being given time to see the city they'd come to protect.

"Ain't Atlanta," Abel said as he and Seth investigated the downtown.

"That where you from?" Seth asked. "You never said."

"Near enough. You?"

"Mississippi. A small place."

Abel asked, "How come you didn't live where your father was stationed?"

"Never worked out to, I guess," Seth answered. "He was out of the country some. Besides, there was a lot of us kids, and where we lived, Mama had my two grandmamas to help rear us up."

"That why you join the army, to get out from three women bossing you?"

"No. I just wanted to," Seth said. "How come you did?"

"Better than jail," Abel answered, in a tone that gave no hint whether he was joking. "Hey, ain't that Sarge and his buddies heading this way? Let's go, before they see us and think of some reason to send us back to camp."

He and Seth turned up a street with vacant lots and then warehouses farther on. Smoke made everything look blurry the same way fog would have.

Seth didn't like the smoke. It made him feel uneasy.

Back at American Lake, once he'd got over being angry about the latrine ditch, he'd almost eagerly latched on to the idea of fighting fires. He'd thought it would be the kind of hard, stick-to-it battle he could shine at, and it wouldn't be a practice battle either.

But he hadn't expected things to start out like this, with an enemy he could feel and smell but not see.

"Abel," he said, "you scared at all? Of the fires?"

"Scared!" Abel said. "I can hardly wait! I saw a big fire once, city blocks burning, people going crazy."

"You liked that?" Seth thought he must be misunderstanding. "Why?" he asked as Abel hushed him.

Nodding toward three threatening-looking men moving in on a young couple down the street, Abel said, "Look yonder. I'd guess that white boy's about to meet trouble."

Wallace

August 15, Afternoon

"Why are we turning back?" Lizbeth asked.

Jarrett answered, "I think we ought to go where there's more people."

From behind them came the shout, "Hey! Ain't that the ranger's little brother?"

Lizbeth felt Jarrett's grip tighten as he hurried her along.

Running footsteps closed in and the same voice, right behind them now, called, "It *is* him!"

Lizbeth glanced over her shoulder and saw that all three men had come within a few feet. The nearest, a man with a scar and one crossed eye, sidled close to Jarrett. "You hear Tully and me spent a night in jail because of your brother? That weren't nice of him, sending us to jail over nothing."

Jarrett's face went taut with anger, but he glanced at Lizbeth and didn't say anything.

"No, it made Tully right mad," the man went on, matching his walk to theirs. "Say, you seen your brother's place lately? 'Cause Tully was saying how pretty a ranger station would look all done up in orange."

Frightened, Lizbeth wished they were closer to downtown and other people. Where they were now the only possible assistance was two young soldiers on the other side of the street.

"Or maybe Tully decided to visit your daddy first," the horrible man was saying. "Take grievances in order, so to speak. How 'bout it, junior, when's the last time you heard how your daddy's doing?"

Jarrett released Lizbeth's elbow then. "Go on," he told her. "Now. I'll catch up."

"But..."

"Now."

She started walking but heard Jarrett say, "I want to know what you're threatening."

"So you can do what?" the man asked. "Help your daddy like you helped your brother out in the woods?" He laughed. "You learned to walk without tripping yet?"

Lizbeth heard a sharp, pained exclamation and turned to see Jarrett reeling, one leg buckling under him. The man who'd been talking kicked Jarrett's other leg, right behind the knee, and Jarrett fell forward. One of the other men caught him and shoved him back to the scar-faced man, and then all three were on him.

Lizbeth screamed.

Wallace

◆

August 15, Afternoon

"Let's go," Seth said, breaking into a run. The white boy was on the ground now, getting his ribs kicked.

The girl tore by, going the other way, skirts jerked up. "I'll bring help," she called as she passed Seth.

Reaching the men, Seth grabbed the arm of the nearest one and ordered, "Let him up."

The man whirled around and, seeing Seth, said, "Soldiers! Let's get out of here."

But then one of his companions, a vicious-looking man with a scar on his face and something wrong with his eyes, said, "Just one, and he don't look like no soldier. He's the wrong color."

Where was Abel? Seth turned for a quick look behind but couldn't spot his friend.

"Bet he stole that uniform," the scar-faced man said.

Ignoring him, Seth reached down to give the white boy a hand up. As he did, a boot toe slammed into Seth's temple, knocking him from his feet and sending pain shooting through him. For a moment he was blinded, and when his vision came back he saw a booted leg pulling back to kick again.

In the next instant the white boy rolled over and grabbed
the man's other leg, and Seth's attacker was swept backward,
bellowing with rage. The man's companions laughed at the
sight before turning on Seth and the boy again. *We're in for it
now*, Seth thought.

Then a whistle blew sharply and Seth heard shouts and
the sound of running feet, and the three men took off.

Still dazed, he watched soldiers rushing up; saw Sarge
swiftly swinging toward him on crutches, the girl by his side.

Sarge spoke to the white boy first. "You hurt bad?"

"Just bruises, I think," the boy answered, struggling to his
feet.

"You?" Sarge asked Seth.

"I'm all right. Just got kicked some."

"Sarge, you want us to go after those three?" another soldier asked.

"No, not our job," Sarge answered. "Miss, can we walk
you somewhere?"

"No, thank you," the girl replied. "Thank you for coming
so quickly." She turned to Seth. "Thank you."

"We'll be going then," Sarge told her. "Brown, get back to
camp. Your time off just ended."

Wallace

August 15, Afternoon

Mrs. Marston pursed her lips and wondered what to say to Lizbeth, showing up on the doorstep with this young man who'd clearly been fighting. Surely this wasn't the beau Lizbeth had been so eager to see, waiting in the park for hours yesterday in case he came. Mrs. Marston had sat with her, for appearance's sake.

But, yes, Lizbeth was introducing him. "Mrs. Marston, I'd like you to meet Jarrett Logan."

"Are you a ruffian?" Mrs. Marston asked him. Might as well get her position laid out. Find out where matters stood and let him know her thinking on coarse behavior.

"No, ma'am," he said, a smile beginning and then turning into a wince. A fresh line of blood broke out from a cut near his mouth.

"For heaven's sake, Mrs. Marston," Lizbeth said, "Jarrett got jumped on by a whole gang of men that ought to be in jail, and if it weren't for some soldiers, he'd probably have wound up dead. I told him you'd help."

"I didn't say I wouldn't. But, Lizbeth, . . . you're all right?"

Mrs. Marston hated asking as much as she knew Lizbeth
hated being fussed over. But she did care for the girl so
much... more than she'd ever tell her. Too much softness ru-
ined a girl quicker than anything, in her experience.

"Yes, Mrs. Marston," Lizbeth said, giving her a quick hug,
not seeming to mind that Mrs. Marston had no idea how to
return it. "I am fine, truly. It's just Jarrett that's not. He needs
cleaning up."

"Then why aren't we in the kitchen heating water?" Mrs.
Marston led the way, knowing the two would follow. She remembered all the times Mr. Marston had shown up with
black eyes and bruises that needed tending. Good man that
he was, he had been a brawler.

Lizbeth, who had brought Mrs. Marston's sewing basket
from the parlor, told Jarrett, "While you're washing, I'll sew
your shirt where it's ripped."

"No need," he said, looking embarrassed. "I can do it
later."

Probably thinks neither of us has ever seen a man's chest! Mrs.
Marston thought.

"Lizbeth, go wait in the front room," she ordered. "Jarrett,
take that shirt off and hand it over. I sew a straighter seam
than she does anyway."

Wallace

August 15, Afternoon

Lizbeth couldn't believe how fast the next hours went. Mrs. Marston fed them lunch and urged cake and cookies on Jarrett, all the while saying she didn't know what the Forest Service was coming to, starving firefighters the way it did.

Finally Lizbeth came right out and said, "I think he looks just fine."

Jarrett, beet red under their scrutiny, looked as if he wanted to sink through the floor.

"Well," Mrs. Marston said, "I just hope he has strength enough to see you home." She turned to him. "You are intending to see Lizbeth gets safely home?"

"Yes, ma'am."

"There's no need," Lizbeth protested. "It's too far for him to walk."

"That's not a problem," Jarrett said. "Yes, Mrs. Marston, I'll see her home."

"And you, Lizbeth," Mrs. Marston said, "you tell Celia to stop being a fool, staying in the woods, just asking to get the both of you burned up. You tell her your room's waiting. You

can call it a visit and not owe a thing. And she won't have
to cook either, since the Forest Service has taken all my
boarders."

"That's generous," Lizbeth told her.

"You think she'll come?"

"No."

"You tell her there's no place worth dying for."

Lizbeth didn't want to argue, so she kept silent.

"You don't agree?"

"I guess it depends on the place," Lizbeth finally answered. "I don't want anybody to die, not us and not any of
the firefighters..." She shot Jarrett a quick look. "But maybe
some places are worth taking risks for."

Mrs. Marston *humph*ed, her breath exploding out her nose.
"'Risks!' If you plan to live to my age, you better think that
out again, young lady. Now, you get on so you're home before
Celia gets worried."

They left the boardinghouse on foot, leading Trenton.
Once they reached the woods, though, and started up the
Placer Creek trail, Jarrett got on the horse and put out an arm
to swing Lizbeth up behind him.

She knew, even as the miles went by, that they were on a
journey she'd remember. She'd never even been close to a
boy, and now she rode with her hands on Jarrett's waist, or her
arms around him when the trail got steep and Trenton broke
into a choppy quickstep.

Sometimes they rode quietly. Sometimes they talked.

Once, going through an especially pretty part of the woods,
Lizbeth burst out, "I do love it here, all the trees and the

mountains, and how there are animals to watch and birds always singing. You know our canary, Billie? Sometimes he sings so hard trying to answer all the wild birds that he goes hoarse!"

"My favorite thing," Jarrett said, "is in the winter, how pretty the magpies look with their dark feathers, flying against the snow."

"The jays are like that, and I get tickled at how they're always fussing," Lizbeth said. "Sometimes they remind me of Celia and me, squabbling whether there's reason or not."

"You two still aren't agreeing on much?"

"Hardly! At least not about what to do with our place. If something doesn't knock sense into Celia, by this time next year she'll have me stuck in some East Coast front room learning embroidery."

"I hope that doesn't happen," Jarrett said. And then, in a lighter tone, he added, "Though Mrs. Marston did seem to think your sewing could use improving."

"As if your fighting skills couldn't!"

They laughed comfortably. She was glad to learn Jarrett could take teasing as well as give it.

The long ride ended way too quickly, with them getting to the homestead just as Celia was putting supper together. "You'll stay and eat?" she asked Jarrett.

"Thank you," he answered, "but I'd best start back if I want to get to Wallace before too late."

"It will be going on toward the middle of the night anyway," Celia said. She hesitated, threw a quick glance at

Lizbeth, and then said, "If you'd like, you can take a blanket out to the horse shelter and sleep there."

"Thank you," Jarrett said again, "but I've got to report for work early in the morning." He frowned. "I hate leaving you two, though. Coming here, we passed fire crews going to the west fork or heading up the divide. Don't you think—?"

Lizbeth interrupted him. "I'll tell Celia what Mrs. Marston said, but we're not going to change our minds about staying. I think your fire fighting is important, however discouraging it seems to you right now, and I think what we're doing is just as important. To us anyway."

She couldn't tell if he agreed, but at least he didn't say she was being foolish. She liked that about him, that he gave her credit for being able to think for herself.

"Jarrett, if you are really returning to Wallace tonight, you better get going," Celia said. "By the way, though...have you heard any news of your brother?"

"Just that he's been hurrying from one job to another," Jarrett told her. "I don't expect to see him soon, but if I do I'll say you asked after him."

◆

Lizbeth walked Jarrett to the edge of the clearing. "I think Celia could be sweet on your brother, if they got to know each other," she said. "But I guess that won't happen until the fire danger is over."

"I guess not," Jarrett said. "A lot's waiting on that."

"Do you think the fires will get much worse?"

"They could. Everyone says the next week will tell."

Lizbeth felt a quiver of uneasiness. "I wish you didn't have to go back on the fireline. I'm afraid for you."

"I'll be all right," Jarrett said. "I survived both today's fight *and* your landlady, didn't I? Anyway, you're the one I worry about. I wish you and your aunt would do like Mrs. Marston said."

Lizbeth didn't answer. *So he doesn't believe we're doing right, staying on to protect what we can.* She wished she herself felt as sure as she was trying to sound.

She'd thought he might kiss her good-bye—a little kiss anyway. That was something else she'd never done, been kissed. But he didn't.

They parted with a hand squeeze and troubled disagreement between them.

Homestead off Placer Creek

August 15, Evening

"What was that about Mrs. Marston?" Celia asked as soon as Lizbeth returned to the cabin.

"She thinks we're fools to stay here and risk being burned up."

"And I suppose she put it just that way?" Celia laughed, expecting that her niece would laugh with her. Celia never ceased to be amazed at the way their landlady spoke her mind. It amused and shocked her and sometimes made her envious. What would it be like to be so certain of things?

Lizbeth said, "Ought we to consider it, Cel? Mrs. Marston invited us to be her guests—no rent, and you wouldn't have to cook for boarders."

Her niece's unexpected question disquieted Celia. She felt herself being pushed into a corner. First Samuel Logan and now Mrs. Marston was demanding she surrender the plan she'd clung to these past years. And leaving *would* be the same as admitting defeat, whether fire swept through the place or not. Stung that Lizbeth didn't understand, Celia demanded, "And you, too? Do you think we ought to give up?"

"Not give up, Cel," Lizbeth answered. "Just not confuse wanting to keep our place with wanting to stay alive."

"You're being melodramatic."

"No. I'm just wondering what makes you so sure you know better than everyone else what we should do. Are you just too proud to admit you're wrong?"

"That's enough, Lizbeth," Celia said, her voice sharp. "You go stay in town if you wish. I don't need you here anyway, and I'd just as soon you be safe."

"Don't be silly," Lizbeth said. "I'm not going without you." She pulled on her work apron. "I'll put the animals away for the night."

"You haven't eaten supper," Celia said.

"I'm not hungry." Lizbeth headed out the door. "But maybe Mrs. Marston is right about us being fools."

———◆———

Celia put the uneaten meal away. She hadn't been hungry either.

Why does what I say so often come out sounding different from what I mean?

Of course she wanted her niece safe in town, but Lizbeth would never go, not after the way Celia had put it.

And why can't I admit I'm not sure at all about what we should do?

She wished she had some way to bring Tom Whitcomb back to life long enough to end things properly with him. It wasn't right, how he'd left her with this place and his ideas to carry out. It was like he'd left her with a test she had to pass over and over, with every decision she made.

Celia knew it was a foolish test, but what would it say about her if she abandoned it? That she'd been fool enough to marry a man who didn't know how to provide for her?

She grimaced, thinking back on the one time she'd tried to explain that to Lizbeth.

"So provide for yourself," Lizbeth had said. "Or let me. We're not hothouse flowers needing to be taken care of."

"You wouldn't know a hothouse flower if you saw one," Celia had retorted. "I doubt there's a hothouse in all Idaho."

As though that had anything to do with the price of apples, Celia thought, remembering. But at least the comment had been so ridiculous it had set them both laughing.

She took out her small stack of magazines and began searching for a picture that might make a good watercolor. Lately she'd been less and less interested in drawings of women playing croquet on clipped lawns, and tonight she could hardly even stand to look at them. Impatient, she put the magazines down and stepped to the door to see if Lizbeth needed a hand.

Her niece signaled that she was almost done with the chores, and Celia started to go back inside. And then she halted, distracted by a whiff of pine coming through the pervading smell of smoke. It made her think of Samuel Logan's scrapbooks. Maybe he didn't know as much about drawing as she did, but he certainly cared more about his subjects. It showed in every line of his work.

Since seeing his drawings, Celia had started to observe more closely the woods she lived in. She'd found that her trees took on a whole different look when she studied how they were made instead of calculating only their value as cut timber.

Abruptly, Lizbeth's question came back to her: *Are you just too proud to admit you're wrong?*

Not too proud, Celia thought. *Too scared.*

Wallace

◆

August 15, Night

Seth got twenty-four hours' sentry duty, not for fighting but for losing. "Teach you to pick your battles," Sarge said, "and to know when you're gonna need help. Get your rifle."

"But that ain't right," Seth said. "That boy was getting beat up, and..."

"And you with him. You should'a known two can't fight three."

I expected it to be even, Abel pitching in with me, Seth thought, but he didn't say it. There had to be a good reason for Abel not backing him up.

Anyway, even without Abel, Seth's uniform should have counted for something. That's what Seth's father used to say. *Most people respect a uniform, even if they don't like the person in it.*

Seth swallowed down bile, not knowing who he was angriest at, Sarge or those men—or his father, for promising the army would be different from what it was. He got his weapon and reported back.

Sarge glanced at his pocket watch and said, "You're on in ten," and returned to a stack of papers he was going through.

Seth waited, the unjustness of the whole thing gnawing at his insides, until finally he blurted out, "How come you don't go after others like this?"

"Like Abel?" Sarge said without looking up from what he was reading. "I've seen lots like him. Good-enough soldiers as long as it suits them to be. I want men I can count on."

"I don't understand," Seth said.

"Abel's not worth my trouble. You are." Sarge glanced down at his ankle, his face expressionless. "Now, you go on."

———◆———

Seth began the first of the dozens of times he was supposed to walk the camp's perimeter, eyes roving while his face and body pointed straight ahead. When he got around to the darkest side, Abel slipped up next to him. It was the first time since the fight that Seth had seen him.

"Where were you?" Seth demanded. "I almost got pounded into nothing."

"I ran for help," Abel said. "That was just good sense. Only, that girl beat me to it."

"You could have told Sarge how it was."

"And done what good, besides maybe get us *both* guard duty? Buddy, I'll make it up to you."

"I don't need you making up nothing."

They were approaching a lighted corner, and Abel stepped back into shadows. "Catch you next round," he said.

———◆———

When Seth returned to the dark stretch, Abel rejoined him. "It's not me you ought to be mad at," he said. "It's the army. Once you and me are on the outside, we won't have to put up with none of this."

"Who said I want out? Anyway, I got two years to go," Seth
told him.

"You think that matters?" Abel laughed softly. "You and
me decide we want out, then we get out."

"I already said that ain't what I'm after," Seth said. But he
couldn't stop himself from asking, "How?"

Abel laughed again. "Thought that would get you. I got
plans."

"What plans?"

"In time, buddy. In time."

———◆———

As soon as Seth's relief took over walking the sentry round,
the white boy from the fight appeared. He must have been
waiting, Seth figured.

"You're the soldier who helped me today, right?" the boy
asked. "I want to thank you."

"Wasn't nothing," Seth answered.

"It was to me! You get hurt bad?"

"No. Look, I got to report back."

"Then I'll get going," the boy said. "I just came by now
because I've got to leave early tomorrow for a fire camp."
He held out his hand. "I'm Jarrett Logan."

Seth hesitated and then, hoping he was doing right, he
completed the handshake. "Seth Brown," he said.

"Nice to meet you," Jarrett said. "Thanks again." He
started to leave.

"Wait," Seth said. "You said you're going back to a fire
camp? You're a firefighter?"

"Yeah."

"Because, I was wondering what it's like, stopping a forest fire."

"You don't stop them," Jarrett answered. "You just try to keep them from running away. And as for what it's like—it's not been too bad for me, but I haven't been at it long. For some others, though..." He shuddered. "It's not something you ever want to see, how somebody who's been burned looks."

Seth was astounded to see tears well up in the boy's eyes.

"Or how he smells or what he sounds like—" Jarrett broke off. "I shouldn't have said that. Most times, fire fighting is no worse than other kinds of hard work. Just hotter."

"I can handle hot," Seth said.

"Then I reckon you'll be okay. You know what fire you're going on?"

"They said I Company's staying here, and G Company— that's mine—is going down to some railroad town."

"Avery, then," Jarrett said, remembering what Mr. Polson had told him. "That's a division town on the Milwaukee."

"You know it?"

"I used to live there, and my father still does. He's a train conductor."

"Mine was a soldier," Seth said. "Look, I really best be getting back before someone comes after me."

"Good luck down in Avery, if that's where you go," Jarrett said. "I hear the fires all along the St. Joe are heating up, so I know you're needed."

Wallace
◆
August 16, Morning

Jarrett found Mr. Polson already at work when he got to the
Forest Service office at 7 A.M., after sleeping under a baggage
cart at one of the railroad stations. Jarrett told him about the
threats from Tully's friend, about what Tully might do. "I
don't know the man's whole name, just *Tully*, but he was the
same one who..."

"I know him," Mr. Polson said. He put a reassuring hand
on Jarrett's arm. "I'd guess that was bluff yesterday, but I'll
send word down to the Avery sheriff so someone can warn
your father and keep an eye on his place. And I'll warn
Samuel when he returns."

"You want me to go check on the Cool Spring Station?"

"You're needed more on the firelines." Mr. Polson hesitated. "But no one would blame you for going down to Avery
to make sure things there are okay."

Jarrett thought, *And Pop would think I was using the threats as
an excuse to go home. He'd laugh in my face, before slamming the
door on me.*

The force of the anger surging through Jarrett surprised

him, since he'd hardly thought about Pop the last few weeks. He'd been too busy.

"Thanks," he told Mr. Polson, "but I want to see the fire season through, now I'm this far in it." He waited while Mr. Polson studied him.

Then the Forest Service man told him, "Well, like I said, you're needed." He went over to the wall map, where he indicated one of many pins clustered along the drainages feeding the St. Joe River. "Now, this is where you're going to deliver that equipment."

Cool Spring Ranger Station

◆

August 18, Morning

Samuel checked the supplies he'd packed into his saddle-bags. He hated to again be leaving his territory to someone else's care while he helped with fire crews farther out. Maybe one good thing that would come of this summer's wildfires would be the Forest Service getting money to hire more rangers.

Anyone with half a mind could see they were needed, along with a lot more firefighters who actually knew what they were doing.

He worried about the woods being full of men who had no idea how a wildfire might act or how fast one could move. Men who had no idea that the only thing completely sure about any fire was that it was unpredictable.

"Want to see if we forgot anything in the cabin?" he said to Boone.

Inside, Samuel telephoned headquarters to report that he was on his way but planned a short detour by the mail drop and to check on a couple of homesteaders. He fastened the pie-chest door securely so he wouldn't come back to mouse-eaten cornmeal. He squared his stack of scrapbooks.

He knew he was dawdling but couldn't put a finger on just why.

Boone, usually impatient to start a trip, seemed to pick up on Samuel's mood. The big dog came over and leaned against him.

"You uneasy, too?" Samuel said. "We must be turning into a couple of old women."

He thought a moment. "Maybe we should leave a note for Jarrett, in case he gets back here before we do." Then he shook his head. "Guess that's not likely."

The last he'd heard, Jarrett was heading for one of the fires down in the St. Joe country and would probably stay there until rain ended the fire season.

I hope he's all right, Samuel thought, *and that he's with a good crew.*

"Boone," he said, "this isn't getting our job done."

Samuel took a last look around the cabin, and when they went outside, he was careful to leave the door unlocked. Anyone coming through would know they were welcome to shelter.

Homestead off Placer Creek

◆

August 18, Afternoon

Lizbeth wedged a bit of lettuce between the crossbars of the canary cage, hoping Ranger Logan and Celia would smile at how Billie nipped out V-shaped bites. "Of course, apples are his favorite," she said.

They ignored her.

Celia said, "I'm still not convinced Lizbeth and I need to leave here."

"It probably wouldn't have to be for long," the ranger said. "Those soldiers joining the firelines should make a difference, and we're due for a weather turn. I'm just asking you to play it safe."

"I am," she said. "We're safeguarding what we own."

Lizbeth noticed that her aunt didn't meet the ranger's eyes.

Why, Cel realizes she's not making sense! She just doesn't know how to back down, Lizbeth thought. More than anybody's warning had, her aunt's uncertainty made Lizbeth consider whether they might be in real danger.

Ranger Logan, appearing to be near the end of his patience, said, "Some of the homesteaders on Pine Creek felt the same way and ended up having to flee for their lives."

"And some didn't, right?" Celia demanded. "Didn't you just bring me a letter from my friend mailed from over there?"

The ranger raised his hands as though to say, I give up.

Lizbeth got the impression that both her aunt and the ranger had things to say that they didn't know how to put into words.

Instead Celia asked, "May I pack you a sandwich for the trail? I imagine you need to be leaving."

———◆———

Lizbeth watched the color drain from her aunt's face as she read Dora Crane's letter. Then Celia put it on the table and went outside.

For a moment Lizbeth didn't move. She didn't want to think about what she'd find in the letter, because she knew it was going to be an end of some kind. Reluctantly she picked it up.

Kellogg, Idaho
August 12, 1910

Dear Celia and Lizbeth,

This is to tell you we are clearing out from this hateful country. I wish I could leave you with good thoughts, but I have none remaining and just hope you won't ever know what it is to lose all. For forty hours, Nathaniel and the children and I fought the blazes threatening at our place, until they had passed us by and we believed we were safe. Then we slept the

*sleep of the dead. Although I realize it is a shameful thought,
I still do not know if I am truly glad God woke us when He
did, for the wind had turned and that fire come back at us.*

*We escaped with our lives but none else, and I fear
Nathaniel's spirit is broken. Tomorrow we leave for my
brother's farm in the Palouse country below Spokane, where
we will try to think what to do next.*

*I am sorry to write this, but after receiving your loving
letter, I did not wish to leave you wondering. I disremember
the particulars of your circumstance, but if you can sell out
now, for goodness' sake do, and get out.*

Your sad friend,
Dora Crane

Lizbeth's eyes filled with tears as she tried to find in the
letter's bitter words the Dora Crane she remembered. They
could have been written by a stranger, for all they held any
trace of the warm woman she and Celia knew. Nobody, Lizbeth thought, had loved this country more than Dora Crane
had, and now she was telling them to leave while they could.

Lizbeth went outside and stood silently by her aunt. Finally Celia said, "I hope she finds things easier on the
Palouse. At least she won't have forest fires."

FIELD NOTES

While the forests of the Idaho panhandle dried into tinder ready to explode, in the rolling prairie seventy miles to the southwest the wheat growers of Washington State's rich Palouse country despaired for their crops. The ground was dry to the touch, dry if you dug down—dry, it seemed, no matter how deep you went.

Farmers who had thrown themselves against the bad odds of a growing season begun with little moisture knew they were losing their fight. Especially now that July and August had brought intense heat and drying winds to the battle. Looking over their land, the farmers wondered what kind of harvest there could be from fields where dust devils whirled between rows of stunted plants.

If the families of the Palouse talked at all over their suppers those bad days, it might be to say they'd heard the Northern Pacific Railway had canceled trains and laid off men because of crop failures along the line.

Mostly, those farm families had all they could do to worry about their own land and livelihoods. But if they did extend their worry to friends and relatives over in the mountains—if by chance they'd ever lived in the mountains themselves in a bad fire year—they might wonder if conditions weren't coming together for a Palouser.

That was what the old-timers called the gale winds that occasionally formed in the Palouse country and blew into the mountains of Idaho. Such a windstorm might last two or three days, filling noses and throats with dust carried an impossibly long distance, and with smoke from any fires it passed through. When the gale winds of a Palouser blew through woods where fire burned, they could pick up pieces of the fire and shoot them ahead like flaming arrows.

In the days right before a Palouser blew, the people that it would hit usually had no idea it was coming.

North of the St. Joe River
August 18, Evening

Jarrett wouldn't have minded staying where he'd delivered the repaired equipment, but soon after he'd arrived a plea had come to the ranger in charge there for any firefighters he could spare. Jarrett and five others had been sent out early this morning, and they were still searching for the crew they'd been ordered to join.

It would have helped some if the land matched up better to the sketched map they'd been given, or if the trail they were supposed to follow existed as anything more than blaze marks chopped into the sides of trees. They'd about worn themselves out climbing up and down the steep drainages that fed the St. Joe River.

Finally they stopped for supper, taking time to make a small cooking fire. They fried bacon to go with the canned tomatoes they all carried. They made boiled coffee in a couple of the empty cans.

"You think we ought to sleep here?" one of the men suggested.

"Let's push on," another answered. "I'm hoping for a camp with a good cook who'll offer me a bedtime snack of hot stew and fresh biscuits. Maybe some berry cobbler."

"What I'd like is flapjacks," still another put in. "With lots of syrup."

◆

Three hours later they found the spike camp they'd been hunting for located in heavy timber a mile from where it was supposed to be, above Slate Creek.

Even in the near dark, Jarrett could see it was a poor setup. Nobody had bothered to rig any shelters, except for a torn cook's tent. Tools and equipment lay scattered about. No ranger greeted them, only a harried crew foreman who wanted to put them right to work.

"We've been walking all day," Jarrett said. "We could use some sleep first."

The foreman looked as if he was going to argue, but then he shook his head and made a disgusted noise. "So get it." He started away but turned back. "All of you speak English?"

Jarrett and the others nodded.

"Good. Then I can spread you out among all these foreigners I got handed. I need at least one person in each group who can understand me."

After the foreman had gone on, one of the men who'd arrived with Jarrett said, "This is where I quit." He jerked his head to indicate a dozen people gathered at a campfire. "Just listen to that babble and take a gander at who's making it."

Jarrett thought he could pick out two or three different languages. Most of the men in the group wore street shoes and city clothes, and a Chinese man was pulling off slippers. All were too clean to have been on a fireline yet.

The man who'd announced he was quitting said, "You think any of them ever saw a forest fire before? You want to get killed, fighting fire with a bad crew is a quick way to do it."

Avery

◆

August 18, Night

Seth listened to the mumbles and snores of the seven other men in his tent and wished he could fall asleep. But being scared wasn't a thing he was used to, and the feeling shamed him and kept him awake.

The fear he'd first felt on smelling smoke in Wallace had caught up with him on the trip down here, when he'd seen smoke hide mountainsides where flames appeared without warning. The sight had made him feel like he might jump out of his skin.

And then today...

Seth thought back to the morning.

He'd gone to assembly expecting to be put to camp labor the way he'd been the day before. Only, instead, he and the others had been handed unfamiliar tools and told to be sure they had full canteens; they were going to strike a fireline to keep fires east of Avery from reaching the railroad.

"You know what a fireline is?" Seth had asked Abel, as they'd headed out.

"Guess we're gonna find out," Abel answered.

"And how about these things we got to work with? You think somebody's gonna show us how to use them?"

The tool Seth was carrying resembled a pickax, except that its heavy head came to a point at only one end instead of both. The blunted back side flattened out to a broad edge something like a hoe blade.

A Forest Service man who was going out to the woods with them heard Seth. He chuckled. "That's a mattock," he said. "You'll figure it out fast enough when you get fire licking at your feet. But so you know, you loosen stones and dirt with the one side and scrape with the other."

Seth had nodded, turned silent by an image of flames snapping about his legs.

Only, as it turned out, the flames didn't snap around him as much as roll down from above. Their fireline angled along the lee side of a scrubby ridge, and most of the fire was hidden from sight on the other side. Occasionally, though, lone trees on the ridgeline burst into flame, and branches broke off and tumbled down.

Seth's corporal didn't know any more about fire fighting than Seth and Abel did, but he passed on what he'd been told: that they were working in a good spot. The fire climbing up the other side of the hill would slow way down once it got over the top, and after it crawled down to the line they were fixing, it would go out altogether.

"Anybody tell the fire that?" Abel asked, drawing a laugh from some of the sweating soldiers nearby.

Seth, hacking into the hard ground with his mattock, didn't see how Abel could joke.

And as if to prove the fire wasn't something to joke about, a heavy burning log plummeted down and was on them almost before anyone saw it coming. It hit one of Seth's tent mates, knocking him down and leaving him gasping for breath like he'd been hurt inside.

After a party left with the injured man, there wasn't any more laughter along the fireline. Just hot, hard work done with wary eyes trained on the hillside above. Work made unbearably hotter whenever the flames got close enough that the men could feel their heat.

Seth had been so thankful when the day finally ended. And now Seth wondered how the others could sleep.

He kept remembering what that white boy had said about burned people. They got a sound, Jarrett Logan had said. They got a smell.

Was Seth the only one in the tent who knew that? Was that why the other men weren't lying awake?

Before turning in, Seth had asked Abel, "Abel, ain't you scared at all?"

"Buddy," Abel had answered, still keyed up from a walk about town, "I am saying my prayers."

Seth, confused, asked, "You mean, to keep you safe?"

"I mean," Abel answered, "you let me worry what to pray for. Didn't I say I'd take care of us? Remember, we're a team."

After hearing that, Seth couldn't tell Abel about the biggest fears he had—that maybe deep down Seth was a coward and that sooner or later he'd run from a fire and then everyone would know.

What could be worse than wearing a uniform and not having the courage to go with it?

It's not like I'm Abel, wanting out of the army, Seth thought.
*But maybe it would be the right thing to do, to get out of my uniform
for good before I disgrace it.*

He wished he knew what Sarge would say. But Sarge had
stayed in Wallace. His ankle wasn't healing right, and the sur-
geon had thought he'd be better off there.

Homestead off Placer Creek

◆

August 19, Afternoon

The filthy sky lay so close in and low that Lizbeth couldn't see the tree line. Drifting tendrils of smoke made Celia— pacing the clearing in front of the cabin—look more like a ghost than a woman.

We don't belong here, Lizbeth thought. *This is crazy.*

Maybe if the smoke had been this thick and the fire smell this pronounced when they'd woken up this morning, they'd have taken Ranger Logan's advice after all and gone to town.

But instead, the morning air had seemed almost fresh. And when it started worsening again, it did it so gradually that there was never a particular moment when it made sense to say, *There. Now it's so bad we must leave.*

She saw Celia shield her eyes. "Hello?" Celia called. "Who's out there?"

A voice shouted back, "Fire crew," and as Lizbeth hurried to join her aunt, a man emerged from the haze.

"Can you tell us what's going on?" Celia asked.

He stared. "Lady, there's a forest fire burning just over that ridge. Why are you here?"

"We...that is, I thought..."

He interrupted. "You've got ten minutes to get out. I can't have my men choose between taking care of you and keeping themselves alive." As he turned to leave, a loud *craaack* tore the air.

"Wait!" Lizbeth said. "What was that?"

"Probably a tree exploding," he told her. "Make that five minutes." Bits of things—pretty bits, like dusty, huge snowflakes—began floating down from the sky. Ash. "I'm sorry I can't stay to help you."

Celia hadn't moved, and now Lizbeth gave her a little push. "You hitch up the horses, and I'll gather what I can from the house."

Lizbeth ran inside, where she threw clothes and Celia's pocketbook and some cookware onto the bed and bundled the quilt around them.

Glancing through the window, she saw Philly and Trenton skittering away from Celia's efforts to buckle on their harness. Another *craaack* sounded, and another. Lizbeth grabbed the quilt bundle and ran out to help.

Bigger pieces were coming down now, not just ash but pinecones and sticks still ablaze.

When she and her aunt had the horses and wagon ready, they scrambled onto the wagon seat, and Celia snapped the reins. Then she pulled back. "Where's Billie?"

"I'll get him," Lizbeth said, and jumped down and ran to the house.

Then she saw his empty cage, its door still tied back from when they'd opened it to give him flying time. Now he perched out of reach above the suspended shelf.

Lizbeth called to him and grabbed a piece of bread and
held it up, but he didn't budge.

"Oh, Billie," she said, tears in her eyes. "I'll leave the
cabin open so at least you won't be trapped."

Then she fled.

◆

At the creek she and her aunt climbed down from the wagon
long enough to soak their straw hats and cotton dresses.
Celia looked back. "Do you think we'll ever see our place
again?"

"I don't know," Lizbeth told her. "Cel, hurry!"

The next minutes became a nightmare as they raced out
of the narrow gulch through a shower of burning debris. Only
their wet hats kept cascading embers from catching their
hair afire. They clung together, hung on to the wagon seat,
strained to keep the horses from running wild, breathed
through an apron when the air became too thick with smoke
to take in raw.

And then they rounded a curve, climbed a small rise,
rounded another curve, and emerged into air as fresh as they'd
breathed that morning. It seemed unbelievable.

The horses slowed to a walk. Lizbeth saw blood return to
Celia's hands as her aunt relaxed her grip on the horses' reins.

"I could have killed us," Celia said.

Then she leaned over the side of the wagon and was
sick.

◆

Celia said nothing else until they reached the turnoff to the
Cool Spring Ranger Station. "Would you mind if I stopped

by the station?" she asked. "I want to get Samuel Logan's
scrapbooks for safekeeping."

Lizbeth drew in her breath. "Cel, I'm sorry. I should have
brought your pictures instead of pots and pans."

"His are better," Celia said. "I should have told him so."

North of the St. Joe River

◆

August 19, Evening

Lying atop his blanket beneath a darkening sky, Jarrett wondered if the day could have been any more unsatisfactory. It had begun with the crew foreman pointing to the Chinese man and telling Jarrett, "You and Rolling Joe there, re-supply water."

All morning they'd fetched water from a tiny stream, ferrying it a half mile up a shotgun trail, making trip after trip with five-gallon bags on their backs.

"That's your name, *Rolling Joe*?" Jarrett asked once, and, getting a nod, told the man his. He also learned the man spoke English. The boss just hadn't bothered to find out.

They drank scalded coffee and ate undercooked potatoes and bread for lunch. Then they spent several hours on an irritating, sluggish blaze that wrapped the bull nose of a hard-to-work hill.

Dinner had been the same menu as lunch, and then Jarrett had gone to his bedroll hoping for some rest.

Now Jarrett laughed to himself, thinking what Samuel

would say to this outfit. Or what Mr. Polson would say. Or Jarrett's boss from Graham Creek. Or Elway.

"Hey, Logan!" The foreman came over. "That fire is doing something different, and I can't tell what. I want you to take Rolling Joe and a couple of the Italians to see if it's threatening to cross the fireline past where you were working it today. If it is, stop it."

Jarrett stood up wearily. An image of the injured man, Benny, that he and Elway had taken to Wallace came to mind. "I'm pretty beat," he said.

"And the rest of us aren't?" his boss demanded.

"I really don't think I should take a crew out," Jarrett told him. "I've never led one, and I don't have a feel for the terrain or where this fire's burning."

"Nobody's asking you to think or feel, either one," the foreman said. "Just make sure that fire doesn't cross our line."

———◆———

When Jarrett's crew got to the fireline, they found the fire had already crept across it but not gone much farther. Jarrett set everyone to beating back the low flames. The situation didn't seem particularly dangerous, but heavy smoke, combined with growing darkness, kept him from seeing what was going on any distance away.

Visibility decreased further as they smothered the fires that were providing most of the meager light by which they worked. The smoke, which boiled more and more thickly, reeked of pine tar and made breathing hard.

Then, in just moments, a thick, filthy cloud engulfed Jarrett, leaving him unable to see his hand held out at arm's length. Frightened, confused shouts told him the cloud had also surrounded Rolling Joe and the Italians, Angio and Vito.

"Keep together," Jarrett called, frantically hunting for a way out of the smoke. He almost stepped into a low bank of fire before seeing its edges. "This way's blocked," he called, his words choking off in a fit of coughing. He could hear others coughing nearby.

From his right came the dull thuds of a shovel, and Rolling Joe shouted, "Not this way! Not this way!"

"Keep together!" Jarrett yelled again. "All of you, stay with my voice." Not knowing if the Italians could understand him, he shouted their names over and over. "Angio! Vito!"

As Jarrett tried to punch his way out of the smoky cloud pressing in on him, he held tight to the idea that staying together was the most important thing.

He didn't know how long they wandered in the sickening cloud. Sometimes they walked what seemed like a long way before coming to something that forced a turn. Other times they went just a few feet before having to change direction.

Finally, though, Jarrett glimpsed the dim shape of a tree and then those of several more, and he realized the trees had to be outside of the smoke cloud. "This way!" he yelled, his voice hoarse. "Here's the end of it."

Rolling Joe and Vito quickly found him but arrived without Angio.

Cupping their hands to funnel their voices, they all shouted his name over and over, until he, too, finally stumbled out.

And then two more figures, one tall and one small and both looking like scarecrows, took shape in the smoke. As the figures came toward him, emerging into the faint glow of firelight reflected down from the sky, Jarrett realized the smaller was a young boy carrying a charred carpetbag.

The taller one, a man covered with soot from his singed-off hair to blackened boot toes, tripped and sprawled headlong. Jarrett, reaching down to pull him up, saw the man's eyes were swollen nearly shut. *No wonder he tripped,* Jarrett thought. *He can't see.*

"Who are you?" he asked. "And where did you come from?"

The man mumbled incoherently, but the boy answered. "I'm Henry Reese and that's my pa. We got burned out from our homestead..." He counted on his fingers. "Three nights ago."

"You've been walking three days and nights?" Jarrett echoed, horrified. "Were you lost?"

"I was," the boy said, "and I couldn't get Pa to say if he knew where we were." He paused. "Where are we now?"

"Within a mile or two of Slate Creek, I think," Jarrett said. He was lost himself, with no idea how far his crew had traveled in their haste to get out of the smoke cloud. He didn't know in what direction camp lay, or if they were still in the same drainage. He had just a vague sense that they'd moved more downhill than up and that the fire was probably above them.

"We better drop a little farther down and then find a spot level enough we can get some sleep," he said. "Then tomorrow we'll find our way back to camp."

He looked at the five faces around him. *Probably Rolling Joe and the boy are the only ones who understand what I just said.*

He wondered what he could do about Mr. Reese, but Rolling Joe solved that problem by taking the homesteader by the elbow and telling Jarrett, "We'll follow."

Jarrett was relieved to see Angio and Vito nod.

For the next hour Jarrett picked his way by instinct as much as by sight. He did his best to keep his little group moving downhill, hoping he was right in thinking the fire wouldn't be likely to travel downhill after them. He wondered if the others sensed his uncertainty.

He'd half expected that by now they would reach the stream where he and Rolling Joe had got water, but they hadn't. So, perhaps they *were* in a different drainage.

Finally he stopped. "Here," he said, indicating that everyone should lie down and get some sleep.

Jarrett tried to think out their situation, but he was too tired to keep his thoughts focused.

He jerked awake. He should set a guard. *You never, ever let a crew turn in without posting someone to watch for fire.*

That was what he needed to do. . . .

Part
Three

Wallace

◆

August 20, Morning

As he often did when looking at his fire map, Mr. Polson pictured a firefighter. Sometimes the imagined man would be a middle-aged immigrant in shabby clothes, sometimes he'd be a young man out to prove himself, sometimes he'd be a settler carrying a pocket watch with a photograph of his family fitted inside its case. Always, he had ash in his hair and soot ground into his skin, and he was hot and tired and hungry and thirsty, and always, always, in harm's way.

Mr. Polson had found that the worse a fire season got—the faster fires multiplied and the bigger the fire-fighting force grew—the more he had to reduce the fight to numbers and resource allocations and symbols on a map. But in the early morning, before a day could get away from him—that was when he reminded himself of the people behind those numbers. Of the individual firefighters who might be anywhere on the steep slopes or in the densely wooded gulches of the Coeur d'Alene Forest.

His map showed the waterways most clearly. Creek after creek fingered down from the divide, flowing south to the St.

Joe River or north to the Coeur d'Alene. They lined up like
the wrinkles around an old person's mouth. Fires often took
their names from the creeks they burned nearest, and fire
bosses thought in terms of who had which crews on what
creeks.

That pin far to the left—that stood for Lee Hollingshead,
who had sixty men on the west fork of the Big Creek that fed
the St. Joe.

John Bell had another fifty on that Big Creek's middle
fork.

East of John Bell and closer to Wallace, Ed Pulaski was in
charge of 150 men spread out for miles along the divide between the St. Joe's Big Creek and the Big Creek of the Coeur
d'Alene. They spilled over into Placer Creek, where the
Twenty-fifth Infantry's I Company had been sent.

And farther east still were James Danielson with eighteen
men on Stevens Peak, S. M. Taylor with another sixty on the
Bullion fire along the Montana-Idaho border, and Joe Halm
with eighteen men far to the southeast.

Mr. Polson's gaze swung back to Avery. Two pins stuck in
a little to the left of the town's name designated William
Rock's and Ralph Debitt's seventy-man crews, both situ-
ated a half dozen miles up Setzer Creek. The Twenty-fifth's
G Company had been sent to Avery and would also be on the
lines near there.

And of course, northwest of Wallace, Will Morris still
battled the Graham Creek fire.

Mr. Polson shook his head, frustrated that for all his map
conveyed, it left a lot more unreported. It didn't have a pin

for every ranger and fireguard running a crew. It didn't show
the spike camps and makeshift shelters used by men working
far from their bases. It couldn't show the whereabouts of the
firefighters who, for one reason or another, were out on their
own.

His map couldn't say where, at that very moment, the fires
were advancing fastest or dying back. Or where winds were
changing direction. Or where smoke had settled in so thick
that a man could get turned around because he couldn't see
his crewmates or a trail or the top of a landmark mountain.

His map couldn't say where, at any particular moment, the
greatest danger lay or who would have to meet it.

North of the St. Joe River

August 20, Morning

When Jarrett jerked awake again, there was daylight. *The guard. I didn't set a guard.* He looked anxiously about for signs of fire and then relaxed when he didn't see any besides the ever present smoke.

The others still slept. Jarrett wondered how he'd ever come to be responsible for a half-blind and shock-numbed man, a young kid, two Italians who understood only a little English, and a Chinese person who called himself Rolling Joe.

Of all the jobs he wasn't prepared to handle...

One thing was for sure. The sooner he could get everybody to the fire camp and turned over to the crew foreman, the happier Jarrett would be.

The boy whimpered and flung out an arm that landed across Jarrett's chest. Then he opened wide, worried eyes.

"How are you doing this morning, Henry?" Jarrett asked.

"I'm okay. I wish Pa was."

"I think once he gets his sight back he'll get better," Jarrett told him, trying to sound reassuring.

"I got a baby brother, but he's with my ma," Henry volunteered. "They went to Spokane to be safe, but Pa said I was old enough to stay and help him keep our place from burning up." He paused. "It burned up anyway."

"I'm sorry," Jarrett said.

"Yeah, me, too."

After a moment the boy rolled over, and Jarrett turned to thinking about his options. From where he lay he could see a good-sized blackened area studded with partly burned trees halfway up a steep hillside. If he took everyone up there, they'd be visible to a search party and probably safer than here. Jarrett remembered Samuel saying that fires don't usually waste their time on old burns.

Before they set off he'd drop down to the gulch bottom and fill their water bottles, assuming he found a creek down there. He again wished he knew if they were above the gully he and Rolling Joe had pulled water from the day before. If so, they must be well to one side or the other of the spot, because Jarrett didn't recognize any of the surrounding terrain.

Avery

◆

August 20, Morning

Seth's day began at 5:15 A.M., when the bugler sounded reveille. He delayed a moment getting up, wishing he could put off going back to the woods. But the army's morning routine moved along just as sure in the field as it did in garrison on a regular post. He had to assemble with the others at 5:30, make mess call at 6:00, line up for sick call at 7:15 if he wanted salve for his blisters.

There was a different bugle call for each thing, different notes and different rhythms, and sometimes Seth thought how he was probably waking up to the same sounds soldiers were waking up to all over. The sounds his father probably had woken up to at all those posts he'd been on and countries he'd gone to. Seth liked thinking on that better than he liked thinking about the day in front of him.

Drill call was at 8:00 A.M. and another assembly at 8:10. Ten minutes after that he shouldered his mattock and again headed to the fires that threatened the rail line. The fires were hard to get to, tucked away as they were in a confusing canyon of deep ravines and steep, rocky faces. Even from a distance he could see the fires were flaming higher than they had the day before. The smoke churned thicker, clogging his head; a stiff wind ground gritty ash into his eyes and plastered his flannel shirt against his arms.

He set to work where he was told, but it took all his willpower to hack at the fire trench when he saw glowing brands roll down on it. Especially when one of them ricocheted up, searing his fingers with a sharp bite of pain. And no matter how hard he tried not to think about the danger around him, there was no ignoring the bright streamers that flared at the edge of his vision.

One time, startled by a tree torching so close that the sudden brightness almost blinded him, he did turn and start to run away. Then, ashamed, he continued on to a large boulder and stood facing it, hoping anybody who'd noticed would think he'd left to relieve himself.

Returning to the fireline, he saw he hadn't fooled Abel.

"Had enough of this yet, buddy?" Abel asked.

"Of fire? I hope never to see another one," Seth answered, trying to sound tougher than he felt.

"Of the army!" Abel said. He grinned. "Ain't this wind great? Just a little more wind, buddy. Just a little more fire . . ."

A corporal overheard and demanded, "What's that?"

Abel answered, "I was saying we need more fire to show our stuff."

The corporal, looking uncertain, hesitated before replying. "Don't wish it. In fact, just don't talk at all."

After he was out of earshot, Seth told Abel, "You didn't fool him."

Abel shrugged. "So what? You think he's gonna trouble his self over us? I keep telling you, buddy, ain't nobody in this outfit gonna matter to us once we're gone, or do one thing about our going."

———◆———

The winds blew harder and the fire whipped more wildly as the morning and then the early afternoon wore on. And more and more Seth felt like somebody else was slamming down the pick end of his mattock. Someone else smashing blazing chunks of wood into smaller pieces of fire that could be beat out. Because it didn't make sense that a body feeling as sick and scared-weak as his could be doing all that work.

He kept expecting that somebody would make out how frightened he was and call it out so everyone would know. Except, he realized, the fire was making so much noise that not everyone would hear.

And then, just when he didn't see how he could hang on another minute, word passed down that they were going back to town. The fires had become too dangerous to keep fighting.

Abel threw Seth a mocking smile. "What'd I tell you? The army gives up easy."

An instant later a large brown blur of fur barreled between them, knocking Abel off his feet in its frantic charge down the burning mountain. Abel let out a shout of surprise that sounded a lot like fear. "What was that?"

Seth, his gaze following the terrified animal, said, "Looks like you got knocked down by a bear."

Then Seth started laughing, feeling like he might never stop, and pretty soon all the startled men around him were laughing, too. All except Abel anyway.

They got back to camp with Abel still acting like his nose was out of joint, and as soon as the company was dismissed he stalked off to town.

Left alone, Seth paced the length of the army camp on its narrow site between the St. Joe River and a mountainside that ran almost to the water's edge. What space the little line of conical-roofed tents didn't take up, railroad tracks did.

He didn't like how it was only four o'clock in the afternoon and already dark as late evening. This was more of the fire's doing, and the wind's, blowing in smoke so thick it hid the hills across the river.

Watching a train go by, he saw a conductor lighting lanterns inside a passenger car.

It made him think of Jarrett Logan. Hadn't Jarrett said his father was a conductor down here? Seth was glad he wasn't Jarrett, out fighting a fire someplace without even an army camp to retreat to.

Wallace

◆

August 20, Morning

Celia and Lizbeth had slept in their old room at Mrs. Marston's boardinghouse, and now Lizbeth awoke still exhausted and in turmoil over whispered arguments that had lasted into the night.

Celia seemed determined to leave Idaho, whether their place had burned or not. "I must have been crazy to risk our lives that way," she said. "Greed for the tree money—I don't know what else to put my behavior to, and I won't remain in a place that makes me that way."

Lizbeth had tried to reason. "Cel, you're not greedy, and, besides, a place can't make you *be* any special way."

"A homestead made Dora Crane bitter. Anyway, even if you're right about that, I won't keep you in a place that can put you in danger so fast. Lizbeth, don't argue. My mind is made up."

"First thing tomorrow," Lizbeth had said, "I'll walk down to see if the Forest Service knows what happened. Maybe the fire went around us, and our trees are all still standing. Then you'd reconsider, wouldn't you?"

"Didn't you hear what I just said?" Celia asked. "I'm not reconsidering anything except which day we leave."

———◆———

The Forest Service office had no news to give Lizbeth, although one of the women employees did say that Supervisor Weigle intended to ride up Placer Creek to inspect the fire situation for himself. "So you might want to come back this afternoon," she suggested.

On returning to the boardinghouse, Lizbeth shared a late breakfast with Mrs. Marston. Just tea and toast, which was fine with Lizbeth. She didn't want to eat up all Mrs. Marston's food when there wasn't any rent or board money coming in to buy more. The boarders were all still out in the woods fighting fires.

As though Mrs. Marston could read Lizbeth's thoughts, she opened a jar of applesauce and said, "I can feed my own." She dished some out and sprinkled cinnamon on top. "Your starving won't help anybody."

Lizbeth looked at her in surprise, and the old woman gave a little laugh. "Well, maybe you aren't exactly my own," she said, "but you and your aunt are as close to family as I've got. I reckoned that long as you were living on your own place, getting along, that didn't need saying. But now... well, you just tuck it in the back of your mind."

Lizbeth nodded and reached over to squeeze a bony, veined hand.

"Now," Mrs. Marston said, pulling back, "no need to go sentimental." But Lizbeth was sure her eyes misted.

And Lizbeth's eyes teared up in response, or at least she

thought that was the reason. Then the next thing she knew, all the tears she hadn't cried the night before spilled out in a torrent. "I'm sorry," she said. "I'm sorry."

"I'd like to know what about!" Mrs. Marston said. "Making a foolish old woman go softhearted? Or do you aim to claim responsibility for the wildfires?"

"No," Lizbeth said, giggling and then sobbing again. "It's just... coming in yesterday, we left so much fire behind, getting worse. I can't bear to think of our place burning. Not just of us losing it, but of *its* being lost."

She doubted she was making sense, but Mrs. Marston nodded.

Lizbeth went on. "And Jarrett and Ranger Logan are out somewhere, along with lots of others, at least *trying* to do some good, and I can't help. And Celia..."

"Celia what?" her aunt asked, coming into the kitchen. She looked as though she hadn't slept well either.

"I was going to say," Lizbeth answered, picking her words carefully, "that you and I need to find something useful to occupy ourselves with while we wait for news. There probably won't be any coming in before afternoon."

"*Occupy* yourselves! You can help me can tomatoes," Mrs. Marston said. "I got two boughten basketsful that are spoiling while we natter over what can't be helped."

◆

Neither Lizbeth nor Celia brought up the previous night's argument directly, but it was the unspoken current that ran beneath the on-again, off-again talk of the next few hours. Working into the early afternoon, they cut stem ends and bad

spots from tomatoes while Mrs. Marston did the stove-and-
jar work. After a while they had ranks of sparkling, newly
filled jars cooling on tea towels. It seemed to Lizbeth that the
labor had calmed her aunt. Or maybe the thought of all the
tomato mush, stewed tomatoes, tomato soup, and tomato-
and-beef casseroles that she'd be making for Mrs. Marston's
boarders come winter had just plain numbed her.

Come winter! We won't even be here! The thought stabbed
through Lizbeth.

They worked with all the windows open, but the oppres-
sive air of the hot day bore down inside the small kitchen.
Mrs. Marston wavered at her post over the canning kettle.
"Perhaps we ought to stop for lemonade," she said. "We
might take it to the porch..."

She broke off as a puzzling, faint noise started up outside.
The branches of a lilac bush by the back door brushed the
screen and an instant later hit it again, harder. And then
wind rushed through the yard, making Mrs. Marston's garden
plants arch over, spring back, and arch over again. Green leaves
tore away from her maple tree. Warm wind coming in the
open window wrapped the tea towels around the filled jars,
and it blew a paring knife right off the table.

"My word," Mrs. Marston said. "That was some gust."

Celia, going to the back door, said, "Dear god, it is getting
so *dark*."

FIELD NOTES

Fire always gives off heat and light, but it never does so twice in quite the same way.

A given amount of fuel—a tree, a wood door, a leather harness, a gallon of oil—can produce only a finite amount of heat. The variables are time and temperature. The fuel can burn either hot and fast, or less hot but for longer.

Think of climbing a mountain. Maybe you hike at a steady pace, your face sweaty and your legs tired but with your heart pumping only slightly faster than it usually does. You get to the top in two hours. You've expended a moderate level of energy over a relatively long period. Burned perhaps six hundred calories.

Or maybe you jog up that mountain, face flaming, heart working hard, calf muscles straining. You reach the top in half the time while having burned about the same six hundred calories. You just burned them faster, hotter, and with more show.

A wildfire, too, can climb a mountain either slowly or fast.

It can take hours or days to creep up a slope of pine duff and brush. Burning like that, the fire doesn't give out enough heat to cause the forest canopy above to burst into flame.

Or, pushed by wind, the wildfire can pick up speed until it covers that same slope in minutes, tearing along at 1500 or 2000 degrees Fahrenheit. Such a fire throws its furnace blast up and out, no longer earthbound but able to ignite a crown fire that can fly across treetops.

It's a fire blowing up, and it throws off superheated air that races upward.

Down below, other air rushes in to replace the air tearing skyward. And still more air is drawn into motion by the gulping of the fire itself, as it reaches for the oxygen it needs to stay alive.

Now the fire is no longer only driven by wind. Now the fire is creating its own.

———◆———

Firefighters went into the afternoon of August 20, 1910, with no warning that strong winds were about to fan the hundreds of fires burning on the Idaho panhandle and in neighboring forests. The firefighters were too isolated, and weather forecasting too primitive.

But a fast-moving cold front was coming toward them from the west. Along its leading edge, dense, cool air wedged itself under the warmer air it met. It sent the warmer air spiraling upward in turbulent currents that fought and joined one another and that whipped up other winds spawned by other, weaker fronts. From Washington's dry Palouse, the winds roiled and grew and sped ahead toward the Coeur d'Alene.

The firefighters—and drifters and townspeople, settlers and miners, railroad workers and loggers—went about their Saturday activities worried by fire danger but unaware they were in the path of swiftly traveling winds. Not knowing that when the winds hit they would blow those hundreds of fires together, and the fires would turn the winds into a gale.

Wallace

August 20, Afternoon

In Wallace, the women in Mrs. Marston's kitchen ignored the increasing winds as long as they could. Finally, after one especially strong blast delivered a hot ember right to the back stoop, Mrs. Marston put down her long-handled stirring spoon. "My heart," she announced, "is not in tomatoes."

Lizbeth and Celia burst out in laughter that threatened to turn hysterical. Then they helped put the canning things away.

Having skipped lunch, now they ate a late afternoon meal of ham sandwiches and rice pudding. Then Lizbeth said, "I'm going downtown. Would you like to go with me?"

"I believe I had better remain here," Mrs. Marston said.

"I may walk down in a bit," Celia answered. "You go on now, if you want."

The shortest way from Mrs. Marston's to the business district was down a long, steep flight of wood steps built onto the hillside. It was a good thing they had handrails—otherwise the wind might have blown Lizbeth right off them.

The fire threat seemed to have brought everyone out into

the streets. People watered awnings, watered roofs, and huddled in groups, staring toward Placer Creek. The smoke rising up in the southern sky was incredible: a huge, angry, churning thundercloud of black.

Lizbeth hadn't been able to see the smoke cloud from the boardinghouse, where the hillside cut off the view. Now that she could, she was shocked.

And from down here she could see, too, the flames of backfires that ringed the city like some sprawling medieval wall thrown up against marauding hordes.

She found the Forest Service office crowded with people looking for information. She recognized several townswomen, probably with husbands or sons out fighting to keep the wildfires from their homes.

"No, Supervisor Weigle hasn't returned," a harried-looking official was saying. Someone handed him a slip of paper. He read it and then said, "I can tell you the soldiers are pulling in from Placer Creek. The fires have forced their retreat."

"But what about the homesteads?" Lizbeth asked. "And the regular fire crews?"

"Miss," the man said, "I just don't know." He raised his voice. "Folks, I'm sorry, but I have to ask you to give us working room. I'll post any word I get."

As Lizbeth was leaving she saw Mr. Polson motion to her. "I remember you coming in here with Jarrett Logan," he said. "I thought you'd like to know that he's nowhere near Placer Creek." He frowned. "But that's where your place is, isn't it? I wish I could give you good news."

"Thank you," she said. "I did know about Jarrett—his brother mentioned it."

"Jarrett's probably all right," Mr. Polson said. "There's plenty of fire activity along the St. Joe, but as far as we know none poses special problems today."

"I see," Lizbeth said. "Thank you again. Oh! And can you please tell me about Ranger Logan?"

"He's in the mountains west of here. I don't think you need to worry especially about him either. To be honest, the Placer Creek area and Wallace itself are our big concerns today."

Outside, Lizbeth saw an automobile pass by and heard a man say, "There goes the mayor again."

"Earning his pay," his companion answered.

"We better be glad he is," the first man said. "We've got an emergency brewing."

A policeman approached the pair. "All able-bodied men are to assemble at the courthouse," he told them. "We're going to start a new round of backfires to protect the town's flanks."

———◆———

Lizbeth didn't keep track of how long she walked, listening in on conversations being shouted over stronger and stronger winds. Talking seemed to be the one thing everybody wanted to do. Even the people holding hoses, fighting to direct streams of water onto buildings, talked while they worked.

She heard folks contending that everyone was getting stirred up over nothing. They said that the hills around might burn, but the fires wouldn't come into town. Not when Wallace had a fire chief who knew what he was doing, all the town's men available to be firefighters, and endless water from the river.

Others said they really should go home to pack. They'd heard evacuation trains were being made up. Why, they asked, was that being done, if Wallace wasn't in danger?

Lizbeth hurried to the train depots and found that at both the Northern Pacific and the OR & N, crews were linking up odd assortments of railroad cars.

She saw people piling goods along the depot walls—suitcases and trunks, bulging pillow slips, and quilt bundles like one Lizbeth had put together.

"Just in case," one woman told her.

"No doubt about it," a man said, gesturing toward the south. "Once Placer Creek goes, we're next."

North of the St. Joe River
August 20, Afternoon

Jarrett pounded out another of the small fires that had flared up in the burned area where he'd brought everyone. At least this appeared to be the last of them.

Hours before, he'd begun wishing he'd done something different with his men. Maybe taken them all down to the creek, where he'd filled their canteens. From there they might have worked their way to the St. Joe River.

He'd discarded that idea because he'd been afraid it would leave a search party wandering needlessly. But the crew foreman must not have sent one out. Surely searchers would already have found them.

And now it was too late in the day to start such a hike, especially with Mr. Reese like he was.

Jarrett went over to where Rolling Joe was dividing up a hunk of cheese Henry had pulled from his carpetbag and offered for all to share. "I think things are safe for the time being," Jarrett said. "Will you be all right keeping everybody here while I try to find our camp?"

Rolling Joe nodded. "I believe so. Do you think you will have success?"

"I just hope the light holds up a few hours so I can give it a good try," Jarrett answered. Although it was still afternoon, the day had turned as dark as at dusk.

Unencumbered by the others, Jarrett moved swiftly up the mountain. He followed the burn as long as he could, cutting across openings where only undergrowth had been destroyed. Then, when he came on a section where whole trees had burned and fallen, he struck out into the green forest.

The ridgeline he was aiming for turned out not to be a main ridge at all, but just a rim that had blocked his view of higher land behind it. He thought he could make out a sharp peak poking through the blanketing smoke and considered trying to get to it.

Then he reconsidered. The peak, if that's what it was, appeared far away, and already he'd picked up enough altitude that much of the smoke lay below him. A ponderosa towered close by, reminding him of Samuel's lookout tree.

Jarrett began climbing branch to branch, wondering, as he did, where a faint singing sound came from. He scrambled up eighty, maybe a hundred feet—until limbs started to bend alarmingly under his weight. Then, with one arm wrapped around the tree trunk, he leaned out as far as he could and pulled boughs away from his face.

For a moment he was caught spellbound by the beauty of the scene in front of him. Far into the distance the tops of mountain ranges rose above the smoky haze that hid valley bottoms. From up here he could even see the sun, a blood-colored ball in a dirty pink-and-yellow sky.

From so high up he could hear that odd singing sound more clearly. Or maybe, he thought, the sound wasn't so much like singing as like water tumbling over rocks and splattering into a pool.

A sudden charge of wind threw Jarrett off balance, and he had to cling with both arms to keep from falling. Then, taking a more determined hold on the tree trunk, he leaned out for another look.

Something on fire fell in front of him—a brand at least a foot long dropping through the tree.

Where had it come from? Jarrett had barely thought the question when the odd, soft noises he'd been hearing loudened into a sound more like the rush of river rapids. An instant later the noise became a waterfall-like roar so loud Jarrett could feel its force.

And then, out there in the distance, the pink spread from sky to ground, became a pink-and-red-and-bronze mass of color billowing up in the southwest and running toward him. Sticks appeared to be tumbling through the air before it.

Then Jarrett realized they were too far away to be sticks. *My god*, he thought, *those are trees.*

He plunged down from his perch, slipping limb to limb with just enough hold to keep from free-falling. As he descended he caught more glimpses of that pink hell of fire coming at him. It seemed to be jumping ahead of itself, sending great gobs of flame flying through the air, setting afire trees that were great distances apart.

The wind hit again just as Jarrett reached the ground. Wind so hard it threw him from his feet.

The men! The kid! He had to warn them. Sheltered as they were, they wouldn't know what was coming.

He almost flew down the mountain, the wind pushing on his back.

As he ran he planned what to do. They could dig burrows to lie down in, use what was left of their water to wet down their clothes.

———◆———

As Jarrett gasped out news of what he'd seen, the others stared at him more puzzled than alarmed. "A crown fire, more than that, coming at us! We've got to dig..." Thunderous wind cut off his words. Jarrett staggered back as the gale hit him, and the men around him swayed and whipped about like saplings. He saw Mr. Reese scream, but the sound of the scream got buried in the wind's roar. "We've got to dig burrows," Jarrett shouted. *"Burrows."*

Henry, eyes wide and mouth open, pointed to the high end of the burn. Jarrett spun and saw it was all on fire again, the unburned tops of the trees ablaze and flames tearing along the ground.

They'd never survive where they were. Fighting not to panic, he thought of Elway's saying, *You can handle what you have to.*

With fire above and on both sides, all he could do was try

to get them to shelter in the gulch bottom and hope the shallow water running through it would save them. Samuel had said, *Whatever you do, don't get trapped in some gully.* But sure death lay everywhere else.

"This way," he shouted, and pulling Mr. Reese behind him, he plunged downslope, turning just long enough to see that the others were following. They tore along, running, tumbling. Somehow the little group stayed together as Vito or Angio, Henry or Rolling Joe helped with Mr. Reese.

Down and down they went, dodging as a tree rolled past, its roots scything through the air and its huge trunk snapping into pieces the smaller trees it hit. Fire chased at their heels.

Jarrett saw Angio yell when flying embers set his shirt afire. He saw Vito throw Angio to the ground and smother the flames. Then the two men were on their feet again, running.

Finally they reached the sheer rockslide that Jarrett had walked around when he'd gotten water that morning. The creek hugged its base, and beyond it the gulch widened somewhat. Wedging up the mountainside opposite, a blackened V studded with small trees showed where fire had burned some other year.

They ran down and around the stony expanse and threw themselves into the water. Jarrett lay there for a moment before forcing himself back on his feet. He pulled and yelled at the others to get up, and then he led them, stumbling and terrified, to a position directly beneath the slide. "Lie down as close to the rocks and as deep in the water as you can get," he shouted, although he knew no one could hear.

He took off his wet shirt and went from person to person to

show them all that they should do the same, so they'd have something to shield their faces with.

Rolling Joe was taking care of Mr. Reese, and Angio and Vito had found water deep enough that they could lie with just their faces breaking the surface, their foreheads and eyes molded by wet flannel. Angio had Henry by the hand and was checking that the boy's face was protected. By now, Jarrett could hear the roar of the fire itself as it rushed into the narrow canyon.

A punch of wind knocked him down and almost tore his shirt from his hands. He pulled it over his head and wiggled into the creek bed.

The fire's noise bouncing off canyon walls made a din too loud for the water covering Jarrett's ears to muffle. He shut his eyes and then reopened them, and through the coarse weave of cloth he saw the air turn orange.

West of Wallace

August 20, Evening

Samuel Logan urged Thistle up a rise, hoping to get a better idea of what was going on. The wind was picking up unbelievably fast, blowing first one way and then another, and before the forest had blocked his view, he'd seen a mushrooming smoke column darken the fearsome mustard sky.

He wasn't used to Thistle balking or to Boone sticking close to the horse's legs. His animals' behavior added to the urgency he felt.

Then they broke above the tree line. Thistle crested the hill, and Samuel got his first look at a wave of fire that appeared as wide as the horizon. It was sweeping toward him, a towering, curling overhang of flame. He had never seen anything like it. Never *imagined* anything like it.

Kicking Thistle into a run back down the rough forest trail, Samuel raced to the crew he'd taken over. He reached his men just as Hank Sickles walked into camp.

"Headquarters says I'm yours to command, want me or not," Hank began, but then his grin faded at the desperate expression on Samuel's face.

Quickly Samuel described the inferno bearing down on

their camp. "I'm going to set backfires above a rock out-
cropping I spotted and hope that slows the fire down long
enough to let us get out. Right now, the rest of you wet down
your clothes and blankets, take your canteens, and run. I'll
catch up."

Most rushed to obey, but Hank shook his head. "I'm going
with you. You'll need help."

Samuel locked eyes with his good friend. "I stand a chance
up there," he said, "and some luck with the backfires might
just buy a chance for these men. But not if they got to make
it out alone. There's not a woodsman among them."

He watched Hank start to argue and then think better of it.

He's remembering he's got a wife and kids, and I've neither,
Samuel thought.

Hank gave a quick nod. "Then I'll do my best," he said.
"But if you haven't caught up by the time I've got everybody
safe, I'm coming back."

"Fair enough," Samuel told him. He briefly considered
asking Hank to take a message back to Jarrett for him: tell his
brother he was proud of him.

Except, that would seem like tempting fate—his or Jarrett's, he wasn't sure which. And as for sending word to
Celia—Hank didn't even know who she was, and there
wasn't time to tell him.

"Fair enough," Samuel repeated. "But if we don't get
moving, we're going to give that fire enough time to *walk* in
on us." He reached for Thistle. "And stop worrying! I'd be a
poor ranger if I couldn't handle a little backfire."

Then he rode to meet the front, knowing he hadn't fooled
his friend for one moment.

North of the St. Joe River

August 20, Evening

"What the hell is going on?" someone asked.

"I wish I knew," Elway answered. "If it gets any darker, we're gonna wish we had lanterns to show us the way back."

He and the others were trudging up a narrow trail to their fire camp, where they should find supper waiting. He ought to be hungry enough, after a long day patrolling fire trenches, but he didn't seem to have any appetite.

The way his heart was pounding and his breath hard to catch, he wondered if something was wrong with him. He was getting too old to push himself so hard day after day. Maybe after this fire season ended, he'd start looking for work that didn't take so much muscle and lung. Though what that would be, he didn't know. Swinging a logger's ax, slamming a sledgehammer against a miner's drill, breaking rock for railway bed—when had he ever learned a job that didn't start with muscle and end with aching, sweaty exhaustion?

He wished he'd told young Jarrett to set himself up so people would have a use for what he knew, instead of just for the labor he could put out. Maybe once this fire season ended, Elway would find the kid and tell him just that. That if Jarrett wanted to become more than an old fire bum, he ought to get himself some schooling.

One of the men walking behind Elway said, "At least the wretched wind is letting up."

Elway, who'd been lost in his thoughts, realized it was true. The wind that had been pushing at them all afternoon had disappeared into a moment of odd calm. And then it whipped again, but from the other direction, and its rush left Elway gasping for breath.

Maybe some water, he thought, tilting his head back to swig from his canteen. What *was* going on? The air around him felt ready to explode. And what was that he was hearing? Rolling thunder?

An instant later he placed the sound. He'd heard it once before, when a fire he'd been working had blown up.

He turned to warn the men behind him, but they were flailing away at a shower of glowing bits. And then, beyond them, on the left, he saw a line of trees explode into flame. For a moment he halted, too surprised to move. Then another wall of fire torched up on the slope opposite and still another broke out far below, in the bottom of the overgrown canyon.

Running pell-mell with the others, he tore up the trail in the only direction not blocked by the growing inferno. The conflagration filled his eyes with scorching smoke and his lungs with choking gases and his ears with the pops and crackles of branches burning and tree trunks snapping.

A flaming log rolled down the slope, and he turned in time

to see it sweep one of the men into the burning chasm. Elway paused, realized the man was beyond reach, and resumed running.

The heat on his back became intolerable, and when he glanced over his shoulder again he saw that the flames were advancing much faster than he and the others were moving up the trail. The fire would overtake them in minutes, maybe sooner, if they didn't somehow stop it.

With no place to retreat to, Elway and the men with him turned to meet the pounding blaze head-on. He rammed his shovel under a chunk of burning wood and heaved it into the wild flames. He saw the others fan out to each side as they all desperately tried to hold a line that they might live behind. But the flames burned too hot and too close, and moment by moment the men were forced into an ever tighter knot.

One man broke, running headlong into the raging front.

"No!" Elway shouted.

Elway saw another man, maybe a dozen feet away, collapse as his clothes burst into flames. The handle of the man's pickax, dropped to the burning ground, caught fire.

Elway had one more fleeting thought of telling Jarrett to fear the fire that couldn't be fought. *This is the fire I was talking about.*

FIELD NOTES

As the flames of the great blowup swept across Idaho and into Montana, gathering strength and speed and size, the people caught before them ran to whatever shelter they could find. Railroad tunnels, mine adits, creek beds, caves, storage pits, old barns, gravel bars—whatever was at hand; whatever they could get to. Wherever they could make a stand; wherever they might be safe until the flames had swept by.

On the west fork of the Big Creek, above the St. Joe, Lee Hollingshead led most of his crew to a previously burned area, while nineteen of his terrified men ran to a tiny cabin used to station packhorses.

Men from the John Bell crew on the middle fork took refuge in a homestead clearing, where some of them lay down in a stream and others crammed into a root cellar.

On Setzer Creek, William Rock led his men to a part of the forest that had been burned the day before; twenty-eight men from Ralph Debitt's crew fled to the next drainage. The rest of Debitt's men had heeded a warning he'd sent earlier that they should return to Avery, but those twenty-eight had chosen to ignore it.

West of Placer Creek, Ed Pulaski gathered about forty men who'd been cut off by the flames and eventually got them into a mining tunnel that had a small stream running through it. He dipped water to throw on the burning timbers of the entrance, and he held back at gunpoint those who became so frightened that they tried to bolt.

On Stevens Peak, James Danielson had his men burn over a field of bear grass, and when the flames of the blowup began to reburn what they'd just blackened, they pulled blankets over themselves and waited.

S. M. Taylor, on the Bullion fire, took men into a mine.

Joe Halm and his crew sought refuge on a sandbar at the mouth of a creek miles southeast of Avery.

Will Morris led his men on a nighttime flight from their Graham Creek camp. They hiked through burning forests until they'd put enough miles behind them that he thought it was safe for them to sleep.

And other rangers across hundreds of square miles of rugged wilderness also did their best to keep alive their crews and anyone else they happened to be with.

The fires ravaged parts of forest after forest—the Clearwater, the Pend Oreille, and the Nezperce; the Cabinet, the Kaniksu, the Kootenai, and the Lolo; some of Glacier National Park—but no place suffered more than did the country of the Coeur d'Alene and St. Joe.

No place saw more people die.

Official counts would put the death toll from the blowup at about eighty-seven, but that's a number based on bodies found and people known to be lost. Certainly a true count would be higher. Regardless of the total, the majority—seventy-five at least—died on the Coeur d'Alene. Most were firefighters, untrained temporaries caught when their jobs turned deadly.

Who they were—where they were—what had happened to each man and to all the crews: It would be days before anyone would know the greater part of that.

Wallace

August 20, Evening

Lizbeth returned to the Forest Service office Saturday evening in time to hear someone demand to see Supervisor Weigle. The supervisor, the person got told, still hadn't returned and word hadn't come in where he was. "Though with Placer Creek blown up," Mr. Polson said, "I hope to God he's found shelter. That they all have. There are so many..."

Placer Creek blown up, Lizbeth thought. *Cel's and my place really is gone.* The information seemed unimportant. Because she'd already known it? Because it *was* unimportant compared with the people who were caught in the fires.

"Things are burning up all over..." Mr. Polson looked at Lizbeth a moment before seeming to recognize her. "I'm sorry about your place," he said. "I wish I could take time to talk now."

The evacuation bell began to ring, and Lizbeth was swept up in a rush outside.

She saw that smoke no longer hid the mountains southwest of town. Now, flames sharply outlined them.

Within minutes, as the bell continued clanging and trains sounded their whistles, people began hurrying to the stations. They came first in straggling groups, mothers pulling along children, and then in a swelling throng.

Lizbeth tried to think what to do—her aunt had said she might walk down to check on Philly and Trenton, so Celia might already be in town. But Lizbeth couldn't go looking for her and go after Mrs. Marston at the same time. And of the two, Celia was the more able to take care of herself.

Running against the crowd, Lizbeth hurried to the hillside stairs and climbed them as quickly as possible, squeezing past those coming down. She passed a man packing things into a hole dug in a rose bed while a woman struggled to replace them with items of her own choosing. She passed a young girl frantically calling, "Duke!"

At the boardinghouse Lizbeth saw that Mrs. Marston had gotten herself, creaky bones and all, up onto the roof and was watering it down with her garden hose. "The evacuation trains are going to leave!" Lizbeth yelled, hoping she could be heard over the fierce wind. "You've got to get on board!"

She saw Mrs. Marston start to shout an answer and then lose her balance and slide down the steeply pitched roof into shrubbery. Lizbeth ran to her.

Mrs. Marston, her face pale, ordered, "Help me up," but then her legs wouldn't support her weight. "What an old fool I am," she said, "hurting myself at a time like this! Lizbeth, you take that hose and get up where I was. Only, you be careful..."

"We've got to get you help," Lizbeth said. "And get you on an evacuation train."

"Nonsense," Mrs. Marston said. "I'm not leaving my home."

Exasperated, Lizbeth said, "You told me no place is worth dying for. Didn't you mean it?"

"I meant it for you. Not for me!" Mrs. Marston paused, looking at her house as though she was seeing more than white clapboard and a front window with stained glass panes. She nodded. "You're right, of course." Then her face turned white as the shock of her fall set in.

◆

A next-door neighbor was too busy corralling children to help, but Mr. Denbury, the elderly bachelor who lived across the street, swept clothes off the seat of his one-horse buggy. Between him and Lizbeth they got Mrs. Marston onto it, and Mr. Denbury started for town. There wasn't room for Lizbeth to ride with them, but since the buggy was slowed by the crowd in the street, she was able to keep up with them on foot.

They reached the flat and were headed for the Northern Pacific station when Mr. Denbury called to her that Mrs. Marston had lost consciousness. "She needs carrying to the hospital!" he shouted, pulling his horse into a turn.

And then someone ran by and knocked Lizbeth down, and by the time she'd scrambled to her feet, wagons and hurrying people hid the buggy from her. And then she couldn't find it again.

Mr. Denbury hadn't told her which hospital he meant, but she assumed it was Wallace Hospital, on the west end of town. That was closest.

She ran the blocks to it and found a line of livery cabs waiting to take patients to safety. She didn't see the buggy, and

Mrs. Marston wasn't in any of the cabs. A nurse at the hospital door said no new patients had come in. "Perhaps your friend went to Providence Hospital?" she suggested.

"That's clear on the other side of town."

"Right," the nurse said impatiently. "And without fires threatening to sweep down on it, the way they are here."

◆

Lizbeth dodged between people rushing to the evacuation trains. They lugged coats and pets, boxes and bags, china teapots. She heard snatches of plans they were making—how fleeing wives would send word of their whereabouts back to husbands staying to defend Wallace.

Usually she didn't think of Wallace as being very big, but that night, the way across the city seemed endless.

As she ran burning embers began falling like scattered raindrops, some flying in sideways and some so big they fell straight despite the driving, swirling wind. She saw an especially bright brand fall and then flames lick out from the windows of a newspaper office, and then she heard a roar of explosion. Within moments other buildings had caught.

"The town's afire!" someone yelled.

"We're going to die!" she heard.

"Bring hoses!" a man shouted, and other men rushed to obey.

For a moment Lizbeth paused, caught up in the sights and sounds. Then she started running again. Already the fire was spreading across the city, the winds that pushed against her back driving the flames eastward. *That nurse was wrong*, she thought. *It's Providence Hospital that's in danger.*

When she arrived there, out of breath and with her side aching, she found that a train engine, tender, and caboose had been diverted to where tracks ran closest. Nuns and a doctor were frantically loading patients into every free space. One nun, who was struggling to lift a man twice her size, asked Lizbeth for help.

"I'm looking for a woman who'd have just come in," Lizbeth said, as they hoisted the man onto the back platform of the caboose. "Can you..."

Then she saw Mrs. Marston watching from just inside the car. Slipping in next to her, Lizbeth said, "Thank heaven! I was so worried."

Mrs. Marston looked at her with bewildered eyes.

Lizbeth gave her a quick hug. "Don't worry," she said. "You let yourself be taken care of, and I'll look after things here. I promise." Silently she added, *Somehow.*

Mrs. Marston was struggling to say something, and Lizbeth leaned close to hear her. "Taking care of things is my job," the old woman whispered.

Lizbeth nodded. "I know."

She stayed with Mrs. Marston until the train started moving. Then she jumped off. Although she knew her dear friend couldn't see her, she waved until the train, with its three dozen patients and almost as many nurses and attendants, had disappeared between burning hills.

And now, she thought, *to find Celia...*

Lizbeth joined a surge of people hurrying to reach a train station before fire completely blocked the streets. As she ran she got buffeted about and once spun completely around, so that she got a brief glimpse of the hospital again and of people on its roof wielding hoses.

She reached the Northern Pacific station as the last of the evacuation trains was boarding. Like the train at the hospital, this one was crammed with people, and still more were climbing on. She ran down the line of cars, looking for Celia. At one door she saw men being pulled aboard. Farther on she saw still other men being hauled off and told to stay and fight the fires.

She heard a man try to sell a ticket for a seat to Missoula, and she saw someone else knock him to the ground.

And then someone pulled her arm. "Where have you been?" Celia demanded. "I've looked all over for you. The train's about to leave."

"I'm not going," Lizbeth said. "I told Mrs. Marston I'd take care of things here. Besides, this is my home."

"And you think it's not home to all these women with sense enough to get out before they and their children burn up?"

"When this is over, they'll come back here, and be where their families belong," Lizbeth said. "If I went with you, you'd see we never returned."

A harried-looking conductor told them, "Ladies. Board now."

Celia said, "The only family you and I have is back East, and we better just hope they'll take us in until we can get on our feet."

"Mrs. Marston is family. Dora Crane is, and I bet the Cranes come back, despite everything. And we've got other friends. The Logans."

"Get on the train now," Celia ordered.

"No."

Celia raised her hand as though to give Lizbeth a shove or maybe to slap her into moving.

Lizbeth grabbed it. "Don't," she said.

And then she pushed her way out of the crowd. A man tried to stop her. "Women and children have to leave," he said.

"Leave yourself," Lizbeth told him. "Take my place."

And then she began running toward the center of town, blinded by tears and smoke and confusion.

North of the St. Joe River
August 20, Evening

The conflagration raging through the gulch touched off a stand of snake grass a few feet from Jarrett's head.

Choking and struggling for breath, Jarrett willed himself to stay conscious and keep his wits about him. His heart hit against the inside of his chest, and his eyes and ears felt ready to fly from his head. *If only the noise would let up, the howl and roar.*

Odd, half-formed ideas floated into his mind. Maybe the fire and the wind were the same thing? Or maybe it was hot light and loud noise that were the same?

He groped around enough to feel that cloth still shielded Henry's face. Then Jarrett realized his own shirt had slipped partly off, but he couldn't quite figure out what to do about it. Sometime later he felt it being replaced and patted down over his eyes.

And then, as a fresh wave of flame seemed to suck the air itself out of the canyon, Jarrett gave himself over to just trying to breathe.

Jarrett had no memory of the fire's leaving, but as he became aware that he was now cold instead of hot, he also realized the worst was over.

The night still was lighted by burning trees, but the solid walls of fire had gone on someplace else. As had most of the wind and the noise.

He sat up and tried to ask, "How's everyone?" but the words croaked weakly. He coughed, painfully cleared his smoke-scoured throat, and tried again. "Men?"

Rolling Joe answered first. "Mr. Reese and I are okay."

Then Henry managed, "Me, too. I'm okay."

Vito checked with Angio before nodding. "Okay," he echoed. "Okay."

We've all come through, Jarrett thought. *Is it possible?*

He and the others dragged themselves onto the creek bank, where they shivered in their wet clothes. As preposterous as it seemed to want a fire after the one they'd just been through, Jarrett knew that was what they needed. He and Rolling Joe spent some time finding enough unburned fuel to build one.

With everyone blackened and soaked through and exhausted past coherence, it was hard for Jarrett to tell who'd been injured and how badly. Vito, moaning and cradling a crushed hand, and Angio, with burned eyes, seemed to be hurt the worst. Mr. Reese had gone mute again, and Henry was already asleep.

That left Jarrett and Rolling Joe to keep their little fire

going and watch for burning snags that might roll their way. They sat in silence, gazes roving.

Once, the warming fire flared up bright enough to show Jarrett a dead fish floating down the creek.

He might have cried, if his eyes hadn't been too dry to make tears.

Wallace

August 20, Night

In Wallace, hundreds of people attacked flames that engulfed building after building. They worked in firelight bright as day. Lizbeth heard that the iron foundry was gone and that one of the railroad depots was burning. That the Michigan Hotel was burning. She saw the new furniture store ablaze.

And houses. Flames consumed the homes hugging the canyon walls above the burning east end of Wallace.

Most of the firefighters were men, but not all, and when Lizbeth moved into a bucket line, the men on either side welcomed her with relief. The line snaked along Seventh Street, north-south through the heart of the city. To the east, all the town burned. High on the hills to the west, fires demolished the forests. But between Seventh Street and those hills, a good part of Wallace still lay untouched by fire.

Seventh Street was the line to hold.

Lizbeth handed along a filled bucket, trying not to stagger under its weight. Then she reached to catch the next one, which was being swung to her by the grip of fine-boned hands. She looked up and saw the soot-smudged face of her aunt.

Celia nodded. "You were right."

Lizbeth held in tears she knew had no place in the fire-fight. She wanted to throw her arms around her aunt, but that would have broken the rhythm of the line. "Thank you, Cel," she said as she grasped the bucket handle. "Your help's needed."

◆

By midnight the worst of the weather front had passed through, leaving lessened winds that shifted and blew back on themselves. By then, her muscles throbbing, Lizbeth was struggling to hold her own on the line. Numbed to everything except passing along the filled buckets, she was slow to realize when there was no next bucket coming.

The line started breaking up, with calls of "We've got her stopped." Hardly daring to believe, Lizbeth looked around and saw for herself that the fire's spread appeared checked, at least on this front. And no fires appeared to be burning in the terraced residential section where Mrs. Marston's boarding-house was.

Beside her, Celia sat on the ground and hugged her knees. Down the street a man leaned out of a restaurant door to shout, "Open for business!"

◆

Half an hour later Lizbeth and Celia sat at a tiny café table, drinking hot tea and eating lemon custard pie. Outside, the streets glowed bright with light from the fires that continued to rage through the east end of the city, but in here, candles flickered and threw long shadows. Electricity was out—the poles burned down and the wires melted.

Lizbeth searched for the right way to ask what she needed to know. Not that the question was so hard, but she was afraid the answer might not be the one she hoped for. Finally she just came out with it. "Cel, what did you mean when you said I was right?"

Celia rubbed her hands over her face and then studied her palms. "I'm just grinding in the soot, aren't I?"

"Cel?"

"I don't know. I guess I meant that you were right about my family being here, since you *are* my family, and you wouldn't leave."

"And that this is our home, too? Where we belong? You know that?"

"Don't push me, Lizbeth. I can't give more tonight," Celia answered. But she softened her words by touching Lizbeth's hand.

Avery

◆

August 21, Morning

Seth waited in line to fill his canteen from the lister bag hanging on its tripod in the center of camp. Some men weren't so careful about what they drank, would rather down river water than wait in another line, but Seth liked having drinking water that wasn't going to make him sick.

Abel appeared by Seth's side. "Hey, buddy," he said, as if the bad feelings of the day before hadn't happened. "We got to talk."

"What about?" Seth asked. "And why'd you miss breakfast?"

"I had things to check. Come walk and I'll tell you."

"Soon as I fill my canteen, I will."

"There's twenty people ahead of you yet," Abel said. "Come *on*."

With a sigh Seth stepped out of line.

Abel led the way to a place behind the tents where they'd be out of everyone's earshot. "Okay," he said, "I got this worked out."

"Got what worked out?" Seth asked.

"My plan for getting us free of the army. You know what's happening? This town is filling with people afraid they're gonna burn up. And you know what else? I heard the lieutenant say there's gonna be evacuation trains made up to take everybody away from here."

"You mean we're leaving?" Seth asked.

"You and me!"

"I mean, is G Company moving out?"

"Nope. Them trains will be for civilians only." Abel glanced sideways at Seth, like he was about to share a good joke. "And my plan is, two of those civilians is gonna be us."

Seth stared at him. "Now I know you're crazy."

"Like a fox."

A corporal came around the tent line. "You two! Out front! New assignments!"

"That's another thing," Abel said. "Our job's gonna be to keep order in town today. Like lettin' the fox in the chicken house, Seth, buddy."

———◆———

"What did I tell you?" Abel said once the formation broke up. "You hear how we're supposed to patrol town to see people don't lose their heads 'cause they're scared? See bad people don't go rob good people's houses after the good people leave town?" Abel whacked Seth's arm. "Like lettin' the fox in the chicken house!"

He paused, looking pleased with himself. "Only these two foxes ain't going in to *eat* the chickens. Just borrow some feathers. What you think, buddy? Find us some nonarmy feathers?"

"What I think is you ain't said one thing I can understand," Seth said. "Now you either talk sense or stop bothering me." He hadn't meant to speak so sharp, but it just came
out.

And Abel, instead of getting mad back, said, "You're right.
I'm sorry. Now here's my plan."

Wallace

—◆—

August 21, Morning

Lizbeth woke up disoriented, and then realized she was in Mrs. Marston's parlor. The carved wood settee with its maroon brocade upholstery was as far as she and Celia had gotten when they'd finally come in.

Lizbeth rubbed her neck, wondering if its stiffness came from her sleeping upright or slinging water buckets.

If the water buckets were the cause, she wouldn't complain. This house was standing because the Seventh Street fireline had held.

Quietly Lizbeth slipped outside and around to the back of the house. Below and to her right the whole eastern end of Wallace stretched out as one blackened, smoking ruin. Here and there brick walls poked upright, roofless and incomplete. Here and there flames still burned. And way over there, on that far hillside where dozens of houses had been—nothing was left.

And nothing was left of the trees on the surrounding mountains either. This time yesterday Wallace had sat in the bottom of a lovely green bowl. Now what was left of the town sat in a basin with bleak, black sides.

All our work, Lizbeth thought, *and there's still so much gone.*

At least the center and western part of Wallace appeared unhurt, as did whole neighborhoods like this one.

She felt anxious, seeing so much lost and, at the same time, so much saved. Anxious and empty, as though she was looking at a spectacle too overwhelming to take in.

North of the St. Joe River

August 21, Morning

"There's the river," Jarrett said, thinking it was about the most welcome sight he'd ever seen. He and Rolling Joe, with Henry's help, had managed to walk everybody down the gulch and out of the forest, but it had been hard. Smoking tree trunks crisscrossed the creek bottom, all smoldering traps—he didn't know how they'd done it.

But it was a good thing they had. The wind was strengthening again, and there was no telling what might happen next in those hills. It seemed safer down here, even if the still-green mountainsides just might be fires laid ready and waiting.

Jarrett and the others climbed a low embankment onto the railroad bed and started the hike east to Avery. Henry led his father. Vito, his hurt hand in a sling, guided Angio. Jarrett fell into step beside Rolling Joe.

Soon he began seeing other bands of firefighters also straggling along the river toward town. Some appeared a lot more beat-up than his group.

The worst was a man who latched on to Jarrett and Rolling Joe for a while. He looked half dead, crazy eyes staring out from a face black with burns, eyelashes gone, brittle hair breaking off when he touched it.

"All piled up," he kept saying. "All piled up." And at first Jarrett thought the man was talking about downed trees. Then the man said, "I told 'em not to pack so close. I told 'em if the timber bracing in that mine caught, they'd all die."

"And did it?" Jarrett asked.

"I don't know."

The man hurried to catch up with the group ahead, and Jarrett guessed from the way he grabbed an arm and hung on that he was after another person to tell his story to.

"We were fortunate," Jarrett said.

"Yes," Rolling Joe agreed.

———◆———

Later, when the sounds of a working railroad yard told Jarrett they were almost to Avery, he asked Rolling Joe, "You got a place to go from here?"

"The Reeses will go to Spokane, where Mrs. Reese waits," he said. "Henry asked me to go with them to help. Then, I am thinking, I might come back to see if the railroad has work."

"It probably will," Jarrett said. "It's always needing men." He paused, knowing *needing men* and *needing Chinese* weren't necessarily the same thing. "Say," he said, speaking impulsively, "what's your real name?"

The man walking next to him hesitated. "Li Danian," he said. "If you wish, you may call me Lao Li. It means 'Old Li.'" When Jarrett started to protest, Lao Li chuckled. "Don't worry. It is an honorable way to call me."

"Then I will," Jarrett said.

"What are you going to do now, Jarrett?"

"I don't know, Lao Li. I haven't got past thinking I need to let the Forest Service know we're alive."

The Chinese man said, "It is because of you that we are."

Jarrett, embarrassed at the praise, shook his head. "That's not right," he said. "We all pitched in. But thank you for saying it."

A few minutes later they reached the first buildings on Avery's western outskirts. Passing Pop's place, Jarrett was relieved to see the window shades down and the front door closed. On a day this hot, the shut-up house probably meant he was off on a train run, well away from the St. Joe fires.

The relieved feeling surprised Jarrett, since he hadn't realized he had been worrying about Pop.

The sight of soldiers in town also surprised Jarrett, and then he remembered talking with Seth Brown about how his outfit was probably headed here.

Jarrett said good-bye to his crew and the Reeses outside the soldiers' camp, where an army corpsman was dispensing help as needed.

Wallace

◆

August 21, Morning

At the one remaining railroad station—one *had* burned—
Lizbeth and Celia learned that the eastbound hospital train
carrying Mrs. Marston was feared lost. Sometime during the
night it had picked up additional refugees in Mullan, which
had been bracing for flames sweeping down on that town.
Since then no further telegraphed messages about its whereabouts had come in.

So much was not known. Lizbeth heard someone say
Supervisor Weigle had finally made it in from Placer Creek,
but he'd had a narrow escape. And that Ranger Pulaski had
saved a bunch of men, but he'd got hurt doing it.

Here, men fought the remains of fires still burning in the
smoke-filled city, and others patrolled, watching for flare-ups.
In the light of day, though, and with the emergency at least
for now behind them, they seemed to have slipped back into
thinking fire work wasn't a job for females. Lizbeth's offer to
help got turned down.

Celia was needed more. Hospital beds were filling up with
injured firefighters coming in from the burning mountains,

and a beleaguered nurse jumped at Celia's volunteering to do what chores she could.

The nurse didn't want Lizbeth, though. "You're just too young, child," she said, not unkindly, her Irish brogue thick. "You don't want to be seeing the wounds we'll have in front of us this day."

"Go on," Celia said. "If things get too bad, I'm sure you'll be called on."

At a loss for what to do, Lizbeth wandered through residential streets, where house doors and windows stood open. She watched a pair of young soldiers go from one home to another, knocking and calling, and where they didn't get an answer, they closed things up for the absent owners.

They reminded her of the soldier who had run to Jarrett's aid, and she wondered if he might be someplace about. Since half the soldiers had been sent to Avery, he might be down there.

Avery, where Jarrett was from. Of course, he was off in the woods someplace—far, far away, she hoped, from the fires that had caught the injured men she'd seen at the hospital. *What's happening on the St. Joe anyway? Does anybody know?*

Abruptly, she turned toward the Western Union office, which was open despite its being Sunday. People waited in line to send word of their situation to faraway relatives. Others bunched up to read a list of telegrams that had arrived and could be picked up.

"Why, there's one sent from Italy," a woman said. "Can you imagine? Someone clear across the ocean is worried about us in Wallace!"

"I don't see how you know that," another said.

"It's from Rome. It's to Wallace. It stands to reason," the first woman answered.

Lizbeth saw an employee come out and hurry toward Forest Service headquarters, a telegram in his hand. She followed him, only to be caught up in the crowd outside the door. Within minutes word of the telegram's contents circulated.

"It was from Avery," she heard. "The St. Joe's burning up. Dozens of dead up Setzer and Big Creek and injured men pouring in."

Lizbeth's whole body went cold.

"How's Avery itself?" someone asked.

"Apparently still safe."

Mr. Polson touched Lizbeth's elbow. "We've got good people down there," he said. "I'm sure they'll have gotten most of the men out."

"But you don't know?"

Mr. Polson looked about a hundred years old. "No," he said. "With communications down all over the Coeur d'Alene, we're lucky to have the Avery line still working. And given all the backcountry between here and there, with trails probably blocked, no way to get word in or out . . . it's going to be days before we know what's happened. Even closer in . . ."

He paused, and when he spoke again his words sounded pained and careful. "We're hearing as many contradictions as straightforward accounts, so it's hard to know what to believe. But we do have several crews unaccounted for, and one of them is a group Samuel Logan took over just the other day."

Mr. Polson shook his head as though wishing to clear it of thoughts worse than he could stand. "Samuel's likely all right, but I thought you might wish to warn your aunt."

Lizbeth realized she must be looking puzzled, because Mr. Polson asked, "Did I misunderstand your aunt's interest? When she came in yesterday to ask about him, I assumed . . . Well, I better get myself back to work. And, Lizbeth, as far as your young man goes—I hear firefighters are pouring into Avery. Chances are Jarrett's safe among them."

Lizbeth felt herself blush. "I don't think he's my young man," she said.

"You might not," Mr. Polson told her. "But he does."

Avery

◆

August 21, Morning

Seth walked patrol with other soldiers up and down the crowded platform of the railroad depot, not sure they were being much help. As far as he could tell, the railroad men were running things the way they wanted to. Or running them, anyway, as much as they could in all this crush of people trying to find out what was going on.

Like Abel had said, outsiders were coming in from all over, adding to the townspeople in the streets.

Seth had finally figured out what Abel wanted to do. Even told straight it sounded mad. Change their uniforms for regular clothes and think they could get away unnoticed?

Seth wouldn't have listened for a minute, except the other things Abel had said were turning out to be true. By midmorning everybody was sure Avery would burn, and everybody knew that only the civilians were going to be sent out.

"It'll work, you'll see," Abel had promised. He'd said how he one time saw a place being evacuated, and how all the people had gone pure crazy with fright. "Crowding and shoving and trying to be the first out."

"Don't you see?" Abel had said. "All we got to do is go pa-trol some empty houses for suits of clothes and whatever else might help us after. Money. Or watches. Stuff like that. Then…"

Seth had stopped him right there. "I'm not doing any thieving," he said. "And I ain't going with you if *you* are."

The instant he'd said those words, he'd wished he could take them back.

"I knew you'd come along," Abel had said. "We're a team."

Seth, smarting from how he'd outtalked himself, had said, "I been meaning to ask about that. How come you just don't do all this stuff by your own self? You don't need me for none of it."

"Just because… 'Cause everybody got to have a buddy. You're mine." Abel had given Seth a hard-to-figure look. "I'm yours. Who else you got?"

Now Seth reached the end of the platform, made a smart turn like he learned in drill, and started back the other way. It was the half of his patrol where he could better see into town.

Lord, there sure was a lot of firefighters roaming about, and they were wearing all kinds of bandages. Mostly around their eyes, Seth saw, thinking fire must be real hard on eyes.

One thing to say for Abel's plan—them not having white skins wouldn't matter in that mob. Right this minute, wasn't Seth seeing a pair of firefighters blacker than him?

And all sorts of people who looked foreign.

Seth turned again and saw two men come around the clos-est corner of the depot. One of them, wearing an engineer's cap, seemed to be having a hard time shaking free of the other. Angrily, the engineer said, "I told you, I don't know where Logan lives. Now stop bothering me." He jerked out of the other man's grip, and Seth glimpsed a hand that was missing fingers.

West of Wallace

August 21, Morning

Something probed at the back of Samuel's neck, an insistent touch that sent pain screaming through him. He tried to say *Stop*, but he couldn't draw enough air up his throat to form the word.

Even breathing was an agony of choking and hacking up grit. He'd got a mouthful of dirt all right, he thought, but that wasn't nearly as terrible as the persistent poking at the base of his skull.

It's bad enough I've failed my pack test, he thought, *letting that mule boot me to kingdom come. That Forest Service man giving the exam has no need to torment me more.*

And why was the man whining? Samuel wondered. He wasn't the one eating dirt.

Samuel struggled to turn his head, the effort causing him to spit up more grit—it tasted like a potato jacket burned to ash in a campfire. *Ash...*

A clearer thought stirred in his mind, and he groped toward it.

This wasn't his ranger's examination, was it? That was years before. And he'd passed it after all. Showed how he could run a survey line, fell a tree where he was told to put it, estimate timber, and shoot a pistol and a rifle. Answered questions. *How would you put out a snag fire? What would you do in a wildfire?*

Run like crazy, he'd written. The Forest Service had hired him anyway. Maybe nobody there had known a better answer.

"Stop bothering me!" Samuel demanded, but he couldn't tell if he'd managed to say the words aloud. Painfully, he swatted at his neck, wanting to halt the hurtful jabbing. He touched sticky fur.

Boone?

Boone surely wasn't at Samuel's ranger examination. Boone didn't come until later, a puppy scraping out survival in an abandoned logging camp Samuel had holed up in for a time his first winter as a forest guard. The little guy had dug himself into a snowbank, and his eyes had blazed fearful and hopeful as Samuel had coaxed him out. Samuel had stretched full out in the snow to do it, just like now.

But that was wrong. Snow would feel good, not like the hot, rocky earth scratching against Samuel. And it would smell clean, instead of like smoke and things burning. If he could just remember...

Snowbank...dirt bank...dirt hollow...

———◆———

The next time Samuel awoke, he knew he lay facedown in the hollow depression he'd dug by the rocks. And he remembered setting backfires, the way he'd promised his crew. As long as he could stand to, he'd fanned the backfires toward the onrushing flames, and then he'd run to the hollow and flattened himself as deep into it as he could. Boone had burrowed in next to him as Samuel had tried to keep his breathing shallow in the thin band of fresh air along the ground.

So we've lived, Samuel thought. He hadn't expected that.

He wondered if his crew had gotten away. And Thistle? The last Samuel had seen of his horse, Thistle was racing in circles, terrified, neighing. A bull elk had run by, and Thistle had shied away from it and then bolted in the other direction as a mountain lion streaked past.

If Samuel could just open his eyes, he thought, he could see who it was that wouldn't leave his neck alone.

Then he remembered that it wasn't a person but Boone who was with him.

They'd need someone to come for them soon, or they would die. Samuel knew that. Die of thirst if not burns.

It took Samuel long moments of worrying over how dry mouthed he was before he remembered he'd saved a canteen of water for just this. And then it took him a long, long time to unscrew the cap and get the canteen to his mouth. To drink some and spill some into his hand for Boone.

Avery

◆

August 21, Afternoon

The scene at the depot was degenerating into pandemonium as more and more women piled onto the evacuation train, dragging children, carrying babies, pulling bags of belongings along.

Hearing someone call his name, Jarrett turned and saw Mr. Blakeney, the railroad man who'd hired and fired him from his job as a fire spotter. Without a word of greeting, Mr. Blakeney demanded, "Logan, where's your father? I need him to help direct these soldiers."

"Isn't Pop on a run?" Jarrett asked.

"No, his run was cancelled, and anyway, he didn't show. First time I've ever known him to miss."

I never have, Jarrett thought.

"When you find him," Mr. Blakeney went on, "tell him to get down here and make himself useful. These soldiers mean well, but they don't know squat about loading trains."

A woman carrying a dog and pulling along a small child claimed his attention. "There's a soldier over there saying no animals. Explain to him pets are different."

"They're not, madam," Mr. Blakeney answered shortly. He told Jarrett, "Get your father," and he disappeared into the milling people crowded six feet deep along the platform. "Order, please," Jarrett heard him call. "In turn, now—women and children only for now. No need to push. No need to push."

Jarrett heard the woman tell her dog, "Don't you worry. We'll just go to a different car." She headed farther up the platform, going in the same direction Jarrett went, and he saw her try to push ahead of others closer to the train.

A voice that sounded familiar said, "Ma'am, you have to step back and wait where it's safe." Jarrett turned and saw the speaker was Seth Brown.

"I will step and wait where I wish," the woman told him. "And I will not have any colored boy giving me orders. Now, move out of my way."

Jarrett watched Seth set his feet wider apart and angle his rifle across his chest. The woman raised her handbag, and for a moment Jarrett wondered if she was going to hit Seth with it, but then a white officer stepped between the two. "Ma'am," he said, "you will follow whatever orders my troops give."

Before moving she called Seth a name Jarrett wouldn't have thought a lady would say.

And then other people shoved by, and when Jarrett next saw Seth he'd moved out of talking range.

The train was about ready to leave. Up and down the line, soldiers were loading on buckets of water and slamming shut windows. They pushed aboard the last of the women, with no more time to do it nicely but just getting them on however they could.

Mr. Blakeney hurried by and then veered back to Jarrett. "Logan!" he said again. "Where's your *father?*"

"I'll go check the house," Jarrett said, following as Mr. Blakeney started on. "But I was just wondering—have you had any news from Wallace?"

Mr. Blakeney briefly turned back. "The talk is, Wallace burned up. If you had people there, I'm sorry."

Jarrett felt sick deep in the pit of his stomach.

A whole town gone? Jarrett thought. *That's not possible, is it?*

But it must be, or Avery wouldn't be evacuating against the possibility of its happening here.

What about the people up there—Lizbeth and her aunt, Mrs. Marston in her hillside boardinghouse? And where was Samuel? Was there an evacuation train for all of them?

Jarrett spotted a Forest Service man and hurried over to ask if it was true that Wallace had been destroyed.

"I don't know," the man answered. "We're getting telegraphs in from there, so something's still standing."

"And Placer Creek?"

A bystander overheard the question and answered, "What I heard is Placer Creek is where the Wallace fire came *from.*"

"Look," Jarrett told the Forest Service officer, "I'm a fire-fighter already hired on. Is there a crew going up to help out? I'll join it."

"Are you crazy? Nobody can get through the fires between here and there, and if anybody needs help, it's us, right here."

Avery

August 21, Afternoon

Abel caught Seth's arm. "You with me? Because I got the clothes."

"I told you, no."

"I didn't hear it. Anyway, why not? I heard that woman not taking your orders. You want to die taking care of things for the likes of her?"

"We're not gonna die," Seth said.

"No? Then why you think all the town folk are leaving this place? Next thing you know, Avery is gonna be deserted. It's gonna be just G Company and the fires."

"Some other men will stay," Seth said, trying to convince himself.

"Yeah. Fools!"

Seth looked toward the mountains. People kept coming down out of them, some in awful shape. Seth had seen one just like what Jarrett Logan told about, a man who had a smell and a sound.

"You saw the women's train go," Abel said. "It barely got

out without catching fire. There's only gonna be one more
train, and then we won't get another chance."

Seth drew in a deep breath. "Where you got those
clothes?"

Avery

August 21, Afternoon

Jarrett found Pop lying close to the kitchen stove, stunned but conscious. His leg was twisted under him, and blood from a scalp wound trickled down his face.

"Pop!" Kneeling, Jarrett gently moved Pop's hair back from the cut. At least it didn't appear deep. "What happened? Did you fall?"

"Surprised a looter," Pop mumbled. "Got away." Then he seemed to register who was talking to him. "Jarrett?"

"Yeah, it's me. Is your leg broken?"

Pop frowned at the question. "Don't know," he said. "I don't think so." He shook his head as though trying to clear his mind. "Jarrett?" he said again. "How did you get here?"

"Long story, Pop," Jarrett answered. "That looter—was it Tully, that brakeman you fired? Because..." Jarrett trailed off, realizing that wasn't what mattered right then. "Look, can you stand up? You can lean on me. We need to get you down to the station before the last evacuation train leaves."

"Tully. That was him," Pop said. Then, seeming to grasp what else Jarrett had said, he struggled upright. "Avery's being evacuated? Help me get my uniform on."

"You're dressed fine," Jarrett told him.

"I'll be needed to work. I must be in uniform."

"Pop! You're hurt."

"My jacket, then. Is all in order at the depot?"

"No, but there's soldiers to keep the lid on."

Pop looked aghast. "Soldiers directing passengers? That's not right. Those soldiers are here to fight fires, not take over railroad jobs."

"Pop, the worry is the town will burn. Now, put your weight on my shoulders while I pull you up. We really do have to make the train out."

Pop groaned as he stood. "Are you going with me? I still don't understand what you're doing here." Anger reddened his face. "I thought I told you not to come back."

"It's a good thing I did," Jarrett said. He got the fireplace poker. "Here, use this for a cane and put your arm over my shoulders."

"I knew you'd show up, tail between your legs. Couldn't handle things on your own, could you?"

Jarrett shook his head. *Poor Pop.*

———◆———

As he hurried his father to the train depot, Jarrett said, "I found Samuel. He's with the Forest Service. Got a ranger station near Wallace."

Pop didn't react.

"He asked after you."

Pop, his face impassive, grunted. It was his only answer.

———◆———

They reached the station as the men's train was almost done boarding. Jarrett got his father into a car, and a soldier saw Pop's injuries and made people move over to give him a seat.

"Bye, Pop," Jarrett said. "Good luck."

"Aren't you coming with me? I asked you before, and you didn't say different."

"I can't, Pop," Jarrett answered. "But once things get back to normal, I'll come visit. Maybe bring Samuel, too."

"You needn't, neither one of you. I told you..."

"Yeah, Pop, we *do* need."

Pop folded his arms across his chest in a way that warded off a handshake, and hugging him was inconceivable to Jarrett.

———◆———

Mr. Blakeney happened by as Jarrett jumped from the train steps. "Why are you getting off?" he asked. "If the fires come this way, there'll be no saving the town and not the people left in it either."

"What about the soldiers?"

"They're still needed here. We'll get them out when we have to." Mr. Blakeney looked impatient. "I can't stand here arguing, but you ought to get on the train, Jarrett." He hurried away.

Jarrett wished he had more time to think. He felt overwhelmed by all that was going on and by how much he didn't know. It didn't make sense that the soldiers were needed but other firefighters weren't. And hadn't that Forest Service man said Avery could use help, if any place could?

It would be so much simpler if Samuel or Elway was here to tell him what he should do. Jarrett had left Avery to start with because he'd understood his duty wrong once, leaving a job he'd been trusted with. He didn't want to get it wrong a second time.

He heard a passenger shout, "Where's this train going?" and an army officer call back, "Missoula, Montana!"

Out of Idaho altogether, Jarrett thought. *I'd be leaving more than my job.*

He walked along the line of cars and spotted the Reeses and Lao Li inside one of them. The train was jammed full by now, but still more men pushed to get on while soldiers fought to keep order.

He saw Angio and Vito crammed up against windows in a forward car.

Soldiers hurried up and down the platform, trying to find space for the men still scrambling to board.

Then a warning whistle blew, and the train started vibrating. Men who hadn't made it into one of the cars now climbed on wherever they could. They clung to handholds on the engine; crammed into the tender. Some even climbed onto the train car roofs, where they clung to whatever they could.

The train began moving with Jarrett still standing on the platform. Well, this was where his wish to battle the forest fires had come from. It would be as good a place as any to see the job through.

He watched the windows of the passing cars, ready to wave when his crew and the Reeses went by.

He got a brief glance of a black face almost hidden under a workman's cap. Jarrett wouldn't have realized that it was Seth if Seth's eyes hadn't happened to meet his. Jarrett saw a flash of recognition in them and then a look of shame.

Avery

August 21, Afternoon

As the evacuation train gathered speed, Seth closed his eyes and leaned his head against the window. He wished he could keep them closed until he was a thousand miles away from anybody who knew who he was. And not just because Abel had said they needed to get away from people who'd recognize them for soldiers.

Used-to-be soldiers, Seth thought. Soldiers slipping away from where they were needed. He was glad Sarge couldn't see him. Glad his dead father could never know.

Deserters. Seth tried out the word silently. It tasted bitter even rolling around in his mouth unsaid.

He wondered if Jarrett had realized what he was doing. Probably, Seth guessed. What other reason was there for a soldier to be hiding away out of uniform?

He felt the train swerve into the turn up the North Fork canyon, and the babble of voices in the crowded car got louder. Then someone yelled just as sudden brightness showed through Seth's eyelids. His eyes jerked open, and he saw flames leaping from a deep gulch on his side of the train.

Out the windows on the opposite side, he saw long fingers of fire reaching out from the hillside, seeming to come right at him.

I didn't get away. I got in worse! Seth fought back panic. He wanted Abel to tell him it was going to be all right. That they'd be through the fire soon, and safe.

Only, Abel was in another car, keeping away from Seth like he'd said he would, so people wouldn't remember them together.

The train plunged into the blackness of a tunnel and then out again into light. And then from underneath came the shriek of wheels braking to a stop.

Someone rammed down a window and leaned out to look. "Tree across the tracks!" he shouted.

A conductor pushed open the door. "I'll need men to clear the tracks," he announced.

He sounds like Sarge giving out work, Seth thought. *Just as calm.*

"You, boy," a man said, prodding Seth. "You look strong. Lean to it."

Seth was closest to the conductor. He couldn't *not* get up without calling attention to himself.

At least he didn't have to take on the work alone. A dozen men piled out with him. They got the tree shoved aside in less than a minute and began the scramble back aboard. Seth, toward the rear of the huddle, swung his gaze across the burning hills hoping to see some end to the flames. Maybe they did give out up ahead, which was what they were all counting on.

And then movement on the bank above him caught Seth's eye. He was almost into the car now, turning to grasp the grip bar and pull himself aboard. *It must be an animal,* he thought, looking back. *Another bear, maybe, running from the fire.*

Except the skittering figure was too small and the wrong color—not a fur color but bright blue.

Seth's heart pounded hard as he realized he was watching a little girl scramble toward the train. "Wait!" he yelled, as a woman appeared behind the girl. She was carrying a smaller child, and as Seth watched, she tripped and the child went flying from her arms.

Seth ran to the spot he'd seen the child land. "Go on!" he shouted to the woman. "I've got this one!"

He heard the train start to move behind him and realized that the engineer didn't know what was going on. Seth grabbed up the child—a little boy—and turned and ran with him, reaching the moving car just as the woman and the girl were pulled aboard. Seth, trotting alongside, handed the child up to reaching hands that swung him to safety. Seth saw the woman take him, but she was looking down at Seth. *Thank you.* He couldn't hear her words, but he saw her mouth form them.

And then that car was sliding past and the next approaching. Men stood at its door waiting to haul Seth aboard.

Seth started to run, matching his speed to the train's and trying to gauge the right moment to jump for those hands. If he missed, he wouldn't get to try again.

I won't get another chance. The scared, fleeting thought that the train might go without him turned upside down. *If I make it, I won't get another chance.*

Seth's steps slowed, and when the waiting men reached for him he shook his head and watched them pass on by.

He glimpsed Abel looking out a window, his face distorted with anger, his mouth saying, *"Fool!"*

Avery

August 21, Afternoon

Avery seemed to have become a ghost town. Almost all the residents had left, and now soldiers patrolled the streets and checked buildings for people who couldn't account for themselves. The soldiers couldn't protect places outside town, though, and Jarrett was sure that some homes and mines in the hills would be looted before they burned.

And burned they would be.

And, probably, the homes and buildings in Avery, along with them.

That seemed increasingly certain as Sunday wore on and fierce winds picked up strength, defeating attempts both to fight the fires and to escape them.

The efforts blurred and overlapped in Jarrett's mind, until he hardly knew which was which.

He and others tried following the Milwaukee tracks into the North Fork canyon, but fire soon drove them back. A man couldn't battle flames that shot hundreds of feet high and covered the width of a gorge.

Jarrett huddled by the river, occasionally slipping into the water to escape showers of burning brands. Clogged with downed trees, the river was a drowning danger in itself.

When night came he watched the entire western sky turn a beautiful, terrible red. Fires burned in the hills to the south, and fires burned behind him and to the north, but it was those wind-fed fires advancing from the west that looked most dangerous.

When it appeared inevitable that Avery would burn, the soldiers and some other men hooked a boxcar behind an engine and left, headed west. Jarrett would have gone with them, if he hadn't been watching the conflagration long enough to know there wasn't any staying alive that way.

———◆———

Seeing a small fire blaze on the edge of town, Jarrett thought perhaps the town would burn *ahead* of the forest fires reaching it. Then he realized someone was attempting a small backfire. *It won't help*, he thought. *Not against what's coming.*

A telegraph operator said he was going to send out word that Avery and the people in it were doomed.

Jarrett believed it.

He couldn't remember why he was still there—why he hadn't caught a train out while he could.

Avery

◆

August 21, Night

Where's everybody gone? Seth fought down panic as he walked Avery's main street. Hot wind blew burning things about and a cat ran by, but he couldn't see any *people* moving in the weird light thrown down from the red sky.

Did they all leave while I was trying to get back? It had taken him hours to work his way out of the fiery canyon after he'd let the evacuation train go on without him. He'd been scared he'd burn up out there without anybody ever knowing what had become of him. He'd worried that if he did make it to Avery, he'd be arrested before he could get back in his uniform.

He just hadn't thought of this—that everybody would be gone away and him left.

I surely messed up this time, he thought. *It won't be nobody's fault but my own if I die here, which I likely will.* He started up the hill to the shack where he and Abel had changed into civilian clothes. *But maybe I can at least do that right.*

◆

Seth, again looking like a soldier of the Twenty-fifth Infantry, even if he didn't feel like one, considered what to do next.

Expecting to die was no excuse for not trying to save himself. Maybe he should go down to the river?

Metal clanged somewhere, but Seth didn't pay it much mind. *Just the wind blowing things.* But then...the noises became too hard and sharp. *More like someone using a sledgehammer.*

The sound seemed to be coming from the rail yards, past the depot. Seth started walking that way, and then he saw the lights of swinging lanterns and began running.

As he neared he made out soldiers moving in the space between a boxcar and an engine tender. And then he saw that the boxcar doors were open and the inside was crammed with men. Men in uniform.

My company!

———————◆———————

They went west, hoping to escape by racing through fire that burned from the mountains, across the railroad tracks, down to the river.

Seth, wedged into a corner of the boxcar, felt about to suffocate from the press of soldiers packed around him; from the smoke, from the smell, from the roar and heat, from the air so acrid he could hardly breathe it.

And then word passed along that the train was almost to the flames, and someone slammed shut the boxcar doors. As the train sped into a place that seemed all terrifying roar, more than a few men screamed.

Seth, staring through cracks between floorboards, saw cross ties burning and waited for the car's belly to catch fire, only it didn't. And then the roar lessened. Someone cautiously cracked open the boxcar doors and then threw them wide.

Another soldier stepped back to let Seth move down to the doorway and take a turn breathing outside air. Seth drew it in, in long, shaky gulps. He could hardly believe that the train had made it through the inferno.

He looked up at burning hills. Looked behind, to where the sheets of flames they'd come through towered so high they hid the mountains. Looked to the curving river, sparkling with the small fires that flickered in the logs floating down it.

He looked ahead, to the fiery trestlework of a bridge they'd have to cross. And beyond that...

"Dear God," someone breathed.

Beyond that was a wall of flame even higher than the one they'd come through.

FIELD NOTES

Sunday night and Monday morning, for seven hours, give or take, the train with the Twenty-fifth Infantry's G Company shuttled back and forth along an ever-shortening length of track. It would go as far as it could one way, until flames at a burning bridge or culvert stopped it. Then it would back up until it was stopped again, blocked in the other direction.

It stopped so men could roll burning trees off the tracks.

It stopped while men cleared away rocks that the fires had dislodged from hillsides.

In the cars men sweated and gasped for air and probably vomited and prayed. Certainly, they must have feared that they would be burned alive, because as each westward shuttle ended a little sooner, it became increasingly clear there would be no escape that way.

Finally, though, just before dawn, the flames behind them, in the east, lifted long enough that the train was able to retreat to where it had started from.

G Company returned to Avery.

West of Wallace

◆

August 22, Morning

Hank Sickles left Wallace at dawn to guide a search party going after Samuel Logan.

Hank had reached town only a couple of hours before, but he'd brought all of Samuel's men with him. A few had minor injuries and all were hungry, but they were safe. Just exhausted from their pell-mell race before a firestorm; from a night spent evading the blazes that sprang up on all sides; from hiking in circles.

They were lucky to be alive, and they knew it. Just as they all knew Ranger Logan's escape plan was the reason that they were still breathing.

All the way in, Hank had hoped to find Samuel waiting for them. Samuel had never caught up like he'd said he would, but they'd had to change routes so many times it would have been easy for him to miss them.

But Hank's old buddy wasn't in Wallace, and no one had heard from him.

At the Forest Service office, Mr. Polson had told Hank to get some sleep while he rounded up a search party.

"I want to lead it," Hank told him, before stretching out on the floor along the back wall.

———◆———

Going on 8:00 A.M. Hank and the other searchers reached the camp area—there wasn't much left but some shovel blades and dented pots—and fanned out from there.

Hank was the one who eventually spotted an expanse of rocks about where Samuel had described. When he saw the remains of a large horse near its base, his heart sank. *What had Samuel called him? Thistle?*

Hank was about to shout for the others when he heard a dog whine. He followed the sound to where Samuel's dog stood over what at first glance looked like a burned log almost buried in charred earth.

Boone, walleyed and hair singed, the tips of his ears gone, tensed to attack, but then tentative recognition showed in the dog's glazed eyes. He stood rigid a moment, seemed to judge, and then he relaxed and let Hank approach.

Hank gently touched the burned form on the ground, intending to say good-bye to his friend. Then he realized that what he'd thought was burned skin was, instead, a badly scorched blanket. An empty canteen protruded from under one corner and an empty water bag from another.

"Samuel?"

Hank felt the figure move.

Wallace

◆

August 22, Morning

Along with everybody else in Wallace, Lizbeth had half expected Sunday's winds to turn the fires back on the town again, but that hadn't happened. Instead, as firefighters continued to stagger in, and rescue crews formed and went out, people had turned to worrying about whether the water supply was safe and where to put the refugees coming in from burned-out mines and lumber camps and homesteads.

Lizbeth wondered what other towns were doing with the refugees they were getting. Word had finally come in that the hospital train had made it to Missoula, and she hoped Mrs. Marston was being taken good care of.

First thing this morning she'd sent Mrs. Marston a short telegram saying that the boardinghouse, Celia, and she were all fine.

Lizbeth was still looking, however, for a chance to tell Celia that Mrs. Marston was safe and to pass along Mr. Polson's warning about Samuel.

Celia, busy at the hospital, hadn't returned to the boardinghouse the night before. So now, Lizbeth went to the hospital to find her and to again offer her own help.

"When I see your aunt, I'll say you're here," the nurse with the Irish brogue told her. This time, instead of sending Lizbeth away, she put a scrub brush in her hands. "If you'll keep after the floors," she said, "I'll be that grateful."

◆

Lizbeth didn't see her aunt until almost lunchtime. Celia, although she looked exhausted, seemed hardly able to hold still long enough to eat a sandwich.

"I'm glad you didn't let me take that train out," Celia said. "What would all these men have done if everyone had left?"

Lizbeth put a hand on her aunt's arm. "I've got something to tell you."

Celia ignored her. "Of course, I'd be more help if I knew more about medical things. I've been thinking that maybe some training . . . once things are better, of course . . ."

"Cel," Lizbeth said. "Samuel's missing."

Her aunt's frantic energy disappeared. "I know. I just helped care for a man from his crew."

"The streets are full of people coming in from the woods. He'll turn up."

"I know that, too," Celia said, sounding as if she didn't believe it. "Have you heard any word of Jarrett?"

"Only that a lot of firefighters who were caught along the St. Joe fled to Avery. I think if Jarrett made it that far, he's likely okay."

"Are they saying how many have died?" Celia asked.

"It's feared dozens did," Lizbeth answered. "But no one knows much of anything for sure."

———◆———

Lizbeth was back scrubbing floors again when she heard a doctor say a telegram had come in last night, and that "the fires have overtaken Avery." She sat back so abruptly she overturned her pail of wash water, causing the doctor to turn and scowl.

She was still cleaning up when she saw Samuel being carried in. She knew it was him because she saw Boone trotting beside the stretcher bearers. Or at least, Boone trotted next to them until the Irish nurse shooed him away.

"Ranger Logan is going to look for his dog," Lizbeth told her.

"Ranger Logan is in no shape to look for anything," the nurse answered. Then she peered closely at Lizbeth. Without commenting on what she saw, she put a wad of salve on a piece of oiled paper. "Why don't you tend the dog's wounds with this," she said, "and then go around back to the kitchen. There's likely a bone or two there."

———◆———

When Lizbeth returned to the ward, she found Celia sitting by Samuel's bed.

"Did he wake up?" Lizbeth whispered.

"Just for a moment. He may not be hurt as bad as it looks. His right hand is burned badly enough that the doctor doesn't know how much use of it Samuel will get back. His only other obvious injuries are burns on his back and neck. It's too soon to tell about his eyes."

Samuel stirred, and Celia reached out to prevent him from turning onto his wounds. "Still no news about Jarrett?" she asked.

Lizbeth, glancing quickly at Samuel, answered, "Not really."

As the nurse had, Celia searched Lizbeth's face. Then silently, she squeezed Lizbeth's hand.

Avery

✦

August 22, Morning

Jarrett felt for the soldiers, having to return to Avery when it was looking like there was a good chance nobody there would live through the day. He'd had the night to come to terms with it, while—at least for a time—they must have thought they'd reach safety.

All the same, he was sure glad to see them. And glad to have something to do.

Everyone's spirits picked up when an officer began directing work that couldn't possibly have been accomplished without the soldiers' help.

Soldiers and civilians scrambled to place barrels about, and dug pits, and filled everything they could with water. They hosed down buildings and patrolled for sparks. They refined plans for the final, gigantic backfire that they were pinning their hopes on.

Jarrett, believing Seth had left town disguised as a civilian, didn't look for him among the returned company. About mid-morning, though, Jarrett glanced across the traces of a water cart he was helping pull and saw Seth on the other side.

I must have been wrong, Jarrett thought. But something about Seth's expression said Jarrett hadn't been wrong at all.

They parked the cart, chocked its wheels, and started back for another job.

"You think we're going to make it?" Jarrett asked, just to say something.

Seth took his time answering. Then he blurted out, "I came back on my own."

Jarrett nodded. "That's what I figured. You get very far?"

"Couple of miles is all, but coming back took time. I was lucky I wasn't missed and that my uniform was where I stashed it." Seth hesitated. "You think I'm a fool?"

"For leaving?"

"For coming back."

Jarrett shrugged. "I don't know. Either both of us are fools or neither is, I guess, since we decided it the same way."

Seth looked puzzled, and then he started laughing. "The last time you and me decided the same way about a fight, you got beat up and I got guard."

"Yeah, I remember," Jarrett said, laughing with him. "We were pretty sorry, I guess."

After that, through the rest of the morning, as the winds picked up, they worked together. They stayed as a team into the afternoon, when the winds blew more and more fiercely. Now and then Jarrett thought of the morning's laughter and for a moment forgot how scared he was.

Finally they helped torch the buildings on Avery's western edge. Jarrett was sad that Pop's house had to go, but it stood right in the area being sacrificed. The plan was to make a backfire as high and hot as possible. The hope was that the onrushing wildfire would draw in the backfire, and then the fires would knock themselves down in a no-man's-land of flame.

It seemed to Jarrett about as reasonable as wishing for the Pacific Ocean to pick itself up and dump itself down on the Coeur d'Alene Forest.

And then there was no more time to prepare. The fires roaring in along both sides of the river were almost upon them.

All around, men stopped what they were doing and edged toward whatever cover they'd prepared. Jarrett and Seth poured another bucket of water over the heavy piece of canvas they'd decided would be their shelter.

Then, side by side, they watched the fires.

On the south side of the river, a set of flames looking as tall as the sky was high rushed down a mountainside and reached across the water toward Avery.

On the Avery side another set of flames that Jarrett knew must have been born of the fires in Pine Creek and Big Creek, Slate Creek and Setzer Creek, roared down a mountain and stretched out to meet them.

For one last moment Jarrett saw the wildfires as separate from one another and separate from the backfire roaring on Avery's edge.

And then there was this . . . *sound*. Jarrett had no other word for it. Like all the air in the world was being sucked away at once. And his own breath got sucked away, too, leaving him gasping to fill lungs that felt as if they'd collapsed. Then a wallop of wind hit him as the wildfires pulled the backfire into them.

Unbelieving, numb with terror, he saw the three fires turn into one towering wall of flame.

A wall of flame big enough to burn up the world, Jarrett thought.

He and Seth dived for the earth and pulled the wet canvas over themselves. Heavy as it was, Jarrett had to hang on to its edges to keep his side from blowing away. He felt Seth fighting to keep the other side down.

I'm going to die, Jarrett thought. *We both are.*

Avery

◆

August 22, Afternoon

The wet canvas stopped ballooning above them, and Jarrett felt its heavy weight drop onto his back.

"What's going on?" he heard Seth ask. Jarrett realized he had *heard* Seth ask the question.

Where has the noise gone? Jarrett struggled to take in what had happened. *Where's the wind?*

◆

He and Seth stayed covered for long minutes more, Jarrett still expecting fire to sweep over them. And then he heard someone cheer.

Not scream in fright.

Cheer.

And he heard someone else pick it up.

He and Seth lifted the canvas from their heads and looked around.

The wind really had quit blowing. The wall of flame, stopped at the edge of town, no longer touched the sky.

Jarrett couldn't have said where everyone found the voices to cheer—not after the night and day of smoke and work they'd come through—but cheer they did. They cheered and they cried.

It was too big a moment to experience alone. He hugged Seth and Seth hugged back.

Men all around them hugged and pounded one another's backs.

FIELD NOTES

Sometimes, miracles do occur.

How else can one explain why, just as those three lines of fire met, the gale that had been blowing for two full days suddenly gave way?

It did happen. At three o'clock on Monday, August 22, abruptly dying wind and the convergence of wildfires and backfire combined to spare most of Avery and all of the defenders huddling inside the town.

And it wasn't just Avery and the people there who were spared. All across the forests of northern Idaho and western Montana, the winds shrank back that midafternoon. They would pick up again and blow fitfully for another couple of days, thwarting efforts to tame widespread fires. But the flame walls had gotten as big as they ever would and were already breaking up. After two days of wild wind, the blowup was over.

The blowup hadn't ended in time to spare all of the Idaho and Montana towns in the line of fire—Falcon, Kyle, Taft, Haugan, Henderson, DeBorgia. Or to spare all of the people, mostly firefighters, that it caught unawares. Deaths on the Coeur d'Alene included the twenty-eight men of Ralph Debitt's crew who'd chosen to ignore his warning. The crews with Lee Hollingshead, John Bell, S. M. Taylor, and Ed Pulaski all suffered multiple fatalities. James Danielson and William Rock each lost one man.

But in Avery that afternoon, those who'd expected to die and then found themselves alive must surely have thought a miracle had happened.

Avery

August 24, Morning

Early Wednesday, Jarrett sought out Seth to say good-bye.

The day before, Jarrett had continued to help with fire fighting until one of the rangers finally told him they had things enough in hand that he could leave if he wished.

He found Seth in a chow line, in the middle of an army camp so orderly it looked like its soldiers had done nothing the past few days but keep it that way. Another private, seeing that Seth had a visitor, offered to hold Seth's place in line.

Once they were away from the others, Jarrett told him, "I'm on my way to Wallace. I'm told the north fork has burned out enough that I ought to be able to go up through there."

"I wish you luck," Seth said. "I mean, with everything."

"And you, too," Jarrett answered, feeling as though there was a host of things he ought to be saying, except he couldn't think of a single one.

Then Seth asked, "What are you going to do once this is all over?"

"I don't know," Jarrett answered. "Stay up there, maybe, if I can work it out. How about you?"

"I reckon the army will tell me," Seth said. "Or do you mean down the road? Probably stay in. I've been thinking about what happened around here—how this was the first time I saw a reason to *be* a soldier, besides that my father was a good one." Seth hesitated, looking embarrassed. "Don't you feel kind of proud about what we did?"

Jarrett nodded. "I do. Look, you want to keep in touch? I could write sometime."

"I don't read," Seth answered. He laughed a little. "Though maybe if I do stay in, I might go to some of those classes where they teach you how. Probably have to, if I'm ever gonna be more than a private."

The soldier holding Seth's place in line called, "Brown, you want cereal?"

Seth put out his hand for Jarrett to shake. "Anyway, you take care."

Jarrett's throat tightened, making it hard for him to say, "Yeah, you, too."

◆

Next Jarrett sought out Mr. Blakeney, who told him Pop had sent word he would be returning to Avery and his job as quickly as possible.

Mr. Blakeney cleared his throat. "Jarrett, about what happened back in July . . . perhaps I judged hastily."

"I made a bad call, leaving my section like I did," Jarrett said. "Anyway, it doesn't much matter anymore, does it?"

"I guess not," Mr. Blakeney said, appearing relieved. "So no harm was done, right?"

"I guess not."

Jarrett left Avery by the route he'd taken only six weeks earlier, but now he found nothing that looked like the green-timbered canyon he remembered. Smoke spirals rose from towering, blackened snags. Twisted rails sank into a charred track bed. Steep ravines were no longer spanned by high, snaking train bridges, although crews were already at work trying to save what was left of the trestles.

The going was so slow that by nightfall Jarrett had made it only as far as Moon Pass. He thought of the last time he'd slept atop the Coeur d'Alene divide. It seemed like years ago that he'd watched dry lightning streak above dense forests and wondered what the next weeks would bring. What Samuel would be like. What fire fighting would be like.

I couldn't have imagined, he thought. *Which, I guess, is just as well.*

Staring into the night sky, his blanket spread on black ground, he wondered what he'd find in Wallace. He drifted toward sleep wondering if Lizbeth was there and if she'd thought of him at all.

Cold awoke Jarrett just past dawn. He pulled his blanket closer around his shoulders, felt something wet brush his cheek, and opened his eyes to a light dusting of snow. Flames that flickered above smoking snags showed against a landscape briefly gone gray-white.

He looked at the desolate splendor a long time before resuming his walk. He wanted never to forget it.

When he reached Placer Creek, he was glad he had the morning's picture in his mind, for here the devastation was less grand and more personal.

He passed a work crew hauling a dead horse from the water, to drag it up a bank where other carcasses were already stacked.

He passed a homestead that he might have missed seeing if an iron bedstead and stove hadn't caught his attention. Black and twisted, they were the only things standing in a small circle of rubble.

He had no need to wonder if there was any chance that the Whitcomb place had survived. Near the turnoff to it, he saw patches where the ground was nothing but ash.

Then, amid all the black, he saw a bit of flashing yellow.

He waited for a few minutes, hoping the bird would fly back into view. He was sure that he was too far from the Whitcomb land for it to be Lizbeth and her aunt's canary, Billie, but it might be somebody else's pet. He quartered an apple he'd planned for his lunch and impaled the pieces on branch stubs.

When he was fifty feet along the trail, he looked back and saw the yellow bird already eating the fruit.

Wallace

August 25, Afternoon

Lizbeth checked in at the hospital, where Samuel Logan was progressing well enough that Celia was again lending a hand with other patients. Lizbeth had noticed, though, that they were all patients in the same ward as Samuel, so that Samuel was rarely out of her aunt's sight.

And, Lizbeth had noticed, now that the ranger's bandages were off, most of the time his eyes followed Celia.

He'd been too groggy to talk much sense during Lizbeth's last visit, but today, after greeting her, the first thing he asked was, "Any information about Jarrett?"

"None that I know of," Lizbeth answered, "but the Forest Service is still trying to sort everything out." She tried not to sound as worried as she felt. "After I buy a few groceries, I'll stop by headquarters and ask again."

Mrs. Marston had wired instructions to open her boarding-house to anyone who needed a place to stay, and now Lizbeth had two families of refugees to see to. They provided their own food, but Lizbeth had begun baking desserts to add to it. The displaced children, especially, seemed to be comforted by the sweets.

———◆———

Since the only things on her list were brown sugar and some walnuts, Lizbeth finished her shopping quickly. Then she paused to read a notice posted at the newly opened relief headquarters on Sixth Street. It said that fire victims might get free meals, help obtaining sleeping quarters, and possibly aid if they were stranded financially. Along the wall donated sacks of coal were lined up free for the taking.

Lizbeth went in and added the address of Mrs. Marston's boardinghouse to the lodging list. "We've two families already, but we can squeeze in more if needed," she told the woman in charge.

It didn't occur to Lizbeth until she was outside again that, technically, she and Celia were among the fire victims the relief headquarters had been set up to help.

Hearing someone say, "Newspaper's out," she went in search of one. It would be the first time Wallace's weekly *Idaho Press* had published since the blowup, and right on time. She joined a crowd gathered in front of a copy that a store owner had hung in his windows.

The main front-page headline said: MISSING MEN LIST NOW NUMBERS 400.

Lizbeth was waiting her turn to get close enough to read the story under it when she heard her name called.

Wallace

◆

August 25, Afternoon

Jarrett had just reached the turnoff to the Cool Spring Ranger Station when he met a work crew going the other way. One of the men on it knew Samuel and said he'd heard the ranger was in a Wallace hospital.

Jarrett felt as though he'd been hit in the stomach. Somehow, as much as he'd worried and as bad as things had been the past few days, he hadn't really feared that his brother would be hurt. Not Samuel, who seemed more able to take care of himself than anyone Jarrett had ever met.

"Is he hurt bad?" Jarrett asked.

The man shrugged.

"Do you know which hospital?"

"No."

◆——————◆

When Jarrett saw Boone on guard by the hospital's front door, he knew he'd found the right place. Someone had put bandages on Boone's ears, and his mournful eyes said all wasn't right with his world. Jarrett rubbed the dog's neck and promised to give him more attention later.

Inside, an Irish nurse with a heavy accent directed Jarrett to the ward where Samuel was.

He found his brother and Celia Whitcomb going through one of Samuel's scrapbooks. When they saw him, they dropped it, and Celia jumped up and hugged him.

"We were so worried!" she said. "But you and your brother want to talk. And then you really do need to find Lizbeth, because she's out trying to get word of you and..." She broke off, laughing warmly. "Anyway," she said, "I'll just let you two alone."

Jarrett left the hospital an hour later, sent off by the Irish nurse, who asked if he'd never heard that sick men need sleep. "And don't you know there's others besides your brother wanting to know you're still breathing?"

———◆———

Jarrett saw Lizbeth give him one quick, disbelieving look, and then she hurtled herself at him, stopping just short of a collision. She put her hand out to shake his, withdrew it, and instead gave him a shy hug. "You're alive!" she said.

"Well, yes."

He hoped his neck hadn't turned as dark red as it felt. There were several people watching. From across the street, Mr. Polson caught Jarrett's eye, grinned, and waved.

"We didn't know what to think," Lizbeth said. "We didn't know where you were, and then first one place and then another seemed the wrong place to be, and..." She broke off. "Where *have* you been?"

"Avery."

"In a *town*! And you couldn't let your brother know you weren't dead? Haven't you ever heard of telegrams?"

"Well, yeah," Jarrett said, "but..."

A man interrupted. "Lad, just kiss her and say you're sorry."

And Jarrett astounded himself by doing just that.

Quick though the kiss was, the crowd at the storefront laughed and applauded. Lizbeth, red-faced, pulled him away. "Jarrett! How could you?"

"I'm sorry," he said. Then he saw that she wasn't really mad. "I mean, I'm sorry I didn't send a telegram, anyway."

———◆———

Friday morning they walked around Wallace, both the destroyed section and the part that had been saved, and Jarrett listened as Lizbeth told about the evacuation trains and the bucket lines.

Jarrett stayed mostly silent as they toured, just once saying, "Burned towns and burned forests look different, but they're both awful sad." They were watching a man pace off the length of a bared foundation. "Though I guess the town will rebuild pretty fast."

"I guess," Lizbeth agreed, as they halted in respect to a funeral procession. "I don't know about all the families, though. People are saying that between Idaho and Montana, the count of those killed is going to be huge."

They walked by the army camp, where Jarrett recognized Seth's sergeant working at a table in the shade of a tree. "Lizbeth," Jarrett said, "would you mind waiting here a minute?"

"Of course not," she said.

Jarrett told the sergeant, "I wanted to say thanks. For what the army's done here, I mean. I don't know if you remember me, Jarrett Logan, but—"

"Oh, I remember," the other interrupted.

"Anyway, that's the other reason I came over," Jarrett said. "It was my fight that got Seth Brown in trouble with you. I can't undo that, but I thought maybe you'd want to know we were together in Avery the day it almost burned up, and..."

The sergeant interrupted again. "Hope you two made a better showing there than you did here."

"That's what I'm saying. I think we did our part, and I didn't see anybody working harder than Seth. Or doing anymore to save things either."

"Of course you didn't," the sargeant said. "Private Brown's a good soldier. Probably one day he'll be wearing sergeant stripes himself. He just don't know it yet."

"Are you going to tell him?"

The sergeant made a noise somewhere between laughter and a snort. "And have it go to his head?"

When Jarrett returned to Lizbeth, she asked, "What was that all about?"

"I tried to do Seth a good turn to make up some for the trouble I caused him," Jarrett answered. "But I think I ended up sounding like I was trying to tell the sergeant how to do his job."

"Did he want to hear?"

"Nope."

———◆———

At noontime they returned to Mrs. Marston's so Lizbeth could make sure that the families staying there had lunch.

Then they put together sandwiches for themselves, and Lizbeth cut the last wedge of a chocolate cake she'd baked. "Would you like to eat in the dining room with the others or take this out back?" she asked.

"Let's go outside," Jarrett said. He wanted her to himself awhile longer.

They spread a red-checkered tablecloth on the back lawn and set out the sandwiches and cake, along with sliced tomatoes and bread-and-butter pickles.

"This is the best I've eaten in more than a month," Jarrett said. "Better than before that, too, since I never learned to make cakes. This is really good."

"Celia's baking is better," Lizbeth told him, but Jarrett could see she was pleased.

They took their time eating and telling each other about what they had done and seen.

Or at least some more of it. There were some parts Jarrett doubted he'd ever tell anyone. What it was like when he and Seth had lain shaking in terror under a piece of canvas, both of them expecting to die. How he'd sat guard with Rolling Joe—Lao Li—in the hours after the blowup, cold despite all the fires still burning around them.

A picture came into Jarrett's mind of him and Elway tending Benny on the train to Wallace.

"What's the matter?" Lizbeth asked. "You look sad."

"I was thinking about a friend, an old guy named Elway. He's missing from a crew that's still finding its dead."

"I'm sorry," Lizbeth said.

They were quiet awhile, and then Jarrett asked, "Have you and your aunt decided what you're going to do?"

"About whether we're going to stay out here, you mean?" Jarrett nodded.

Lizbeth smiled. "We're planning to. Mrs. Marston will need us, and Celia's talking about training to be a nurse.

Though...I don't know...I'm trying to talk her into com-
pleting the patent on her homestead. I expect that with the
fires and all, the government will give us some leeway on this
year's requirements, and if it turns out Celia and Samuel..."
Lizbeth stopped, her face tingeing to pink.

"Will be needing a place to live?" Jarrett finished, grin-
ning. "I doubt Samuel's injuries will let him return to ranger-
ing anytime soon, but he probably knows enough about
growing things to make your place productive, if anybody
can."

"They're sweet together, aren't they?" Lizbeth said, a
comment Jarrett had no idea how to respond to.

Then she asked, "What about you? What are your plans?"

Jarrett hesitated before gesturing toward the black hills
in the distance. "I'm not sure exactly, but I want to help do
something about the forests if I can. They'll take years of
work to restore."

"You say that like you've been making plans," Lizbeth
said.

"I've started to. I want to stay in Wallace this year and finish up high school. And earn some money, too, for college.
Samuel and I talked about it some last evening. He says if I
want to be a ranger, I ought to do it right. Study forestry in a
classroom instead of learning it mistake by mistake."

"I'll like doing our senior year together," Lizbeth told him.
"And then..."

A butterfly flitted in front of them, and its yellow markings
reminded Jarrett to tell Lizbeth about seeing a canary on his
walk into Wallace. "I thought maybe, when you're ready,

we'd go to your place and find out if Billie's waiting to be rescued."

"We should go soon, then," Lizbeth said, "although I hate thinking what it's going to be like up there." She paused. "Jarrett, do you think we'll ever see things looking the way they used to? The forests so pretty and green, I mean?"

Jarrett thought about the miles and miles of mammoth trees he'd seen burned to black trunks and charred limbs. Ponderosas and white pines that had probably taken a hundred, maybe two hundred, years to grow so big. "I guess we'll see woods full of new trees, and that will be pretty," he said. "But, no, it won't be the same. Not any more than any of us will ever be the same."

She studied him a moment. "Jarrett, has anybody said they're proud of you?"

He laughed. "Not unless you count Seth and me bragging on ourselves."

"Because *I* am. What you did out there—the fire fighting and all—it mattered. And you didn't shy away from any of it. As long as I know you, I'm not ever going to forget that."

Jarrett, his throat unexpectedly tightening, paused before he answered. Then he settled for saying, "I hope that will be a long time."

Avery

September 3, Morning

Breakfast was done and G Company was folding up its tents when Sarge came looking for Seth. "I want you to walk me up in the hills," he said. He started off without waiting for an answer.

Sarge had only got to Avery the night before. He'd hitched a ride with a pack train so he could rejoin his company for the trip back to Spokane, to their garrison at Fort George Wright.

Seth had heard an officer tell him, "You could have met up with us there."

"I wanted to see where my men have been, sir," Sarge had answered.

Now Seth gave a worried look toward all the gear still to be stowed away. One of his tent mates told him, "It's okay, Brown. We got it."

And another of the guys joked, "Brown, only you could catch Sarge's eye this fast." He said it the way a friend would.

Seth hurried after the sergeant, who moved pretty good despite still favoring his ankle. "Do you want to go someplace special?"

"Where did you work most?" Sarge asked.

"I guess on the fireline we cut to protect the railroad," Seth said. "But that's out a piece and not easy going."

When Sarge just raised his eyebrows, Seth led off.

And it *was* a hard hike over and around obstacles, and things looked so different, Seth wasn't even sure he had the way right. Finally, though, they reached a spot he thought looked familiar. He reached out a hand to help Sarge up a steep section of makeshift trail gouged into the hillside. A muddy pile of rocks and earth and burned tree limbs lay below: more of the hillside, washed down by the rains since the blowup.

"There's not much to see," Seth said. "I think our fireline is under all that."

"I can see enough." Sarge shook his head and paused. "First time I ever had to let my men go off without me," he said, his voice troubled.

Seth, not knowing what to answer, wished he had something better to show the sarge. "If you want to walk back into Avery, there's more to see," he suggested. "We didn't do much good here in the woods."

"I heard about the firefight in town," Sarge told him. "Heard about you, in particular. That friend of yours—white boy named Jarrett?—he came by to see me in Wallace and said a bit about what it was like here."

Seth's face went hot as he waited to hear what was coming. Had Sarge found out about his running away?

"Anyway," Sarge said, "I understand you did a good job. The officers said so, too. Thought I'd pass it along."

Seth swallowed hard before he spoke. "Thank you, Sarge."

He wished again he had something interesting to show. And then he noticed a couple of landmarks and realized just where they were. "You see that bank up there?" he said. "A bear came down it one day, ran right between me and Abel, and..." Seth's voice trailed off.

"Gone and good riddance," Sarge said. "Though you ever tell anybody I said that and I'll have you digging latrines across the whole state of Washington."

"Yes, Sarge." Seth started laughing. "Sarge, you should've seen Abel, flat on his back and not knowing what hit him."

Seth could remember it all so clearly, the flames and the barreling, terrified animal. How hot it had been. How noisy, with all that wind and fire.

Not like the silence now. There wasn't even a breeze blowing through tree branches to listen to.

Just the *tap-tap* of a bird pecking at a charred, split-open pinecone.

Something whizzed by Seth's ear, and he turned, startled. "What was that?"

"Beetle," Sarge said, pointing to an insect speeding from one burned tree trunk to another.

It picked one to settle on and began exploring the thick, blackened bark.

"I wonder how he got here," Seth said. "Two days ago you could go out in the woods and not find one living thing."

"I guess he flew in, same as that bird," Sarge said. "Must

be some reason why." He watched it a moment before telling Seth he was ready to start back.

———◆———

They were almost to camp when the notes of a bugle call reached them. "Sounds like the colors being struck," Seth said.

"That it does," Sarge agreed. "Time to take our flag and go home."

FIELD NOTES

In Placer Canyon the following summer, soft-petaled spikes of fire-weed brushed a purple smudge across the floor of the scoured forest. Pale green willow shoots waved above a silty stream. The colors broke the bleakness of the blackened snags that poked into the sky and the pencil-like timber that lay every which way on exposed hillsides.

From all directions there came sound—much of it chewing, grinding—a noise like you make when you clinch your teeth and suck air between your tongue and the insides of your cheeks.

It was the sound of countless larvae eating their way through the wood of burned pines. The larvae had hatched from eggs laid in the fall by beetles evolved to thrive behind fire. They'd begun moving into the Big Burn while flames still flickered across the smoldering land.

Other sounds—sharp taps—were made by black-backed woodpeckers digging for the beetle larvae to feed on. More and more of the woodpeckers were coming into the canyon. They would stay for four or five years, while the larvae population remained high, and then move on to another, newer burn.

Sticks snapped under the hooves of a browsing deer and her fawn. The doe, head down, nudged away cinders to nibble at green plants that thrust up among them.

And a large, mostly gray bird looked up to call out a grating kraaa. *Then it went back to work, pecking at a pinecone.*

It was a Clark's nutcracker, and it was harvesting ponderosa seeds, storing them in a pouch under its tongue. Once it gathered several—as many as 150 seeds could fit in the pouch—it would search out a bare patch of ground and bury them there to be food for the next nesting season.

Only, when the bird returned to retrieve them in March or April, it would almost certainly miss a few.

Some of those missed seeds would sprout in earth that fire had opened to the sun. And some seedlings would grow into trees.

But long before any of that happened, across the Coeur d'Alene railroads would be running again, ranger stations busy, mines reopening, rebuilding begun—people reclaiming the Big Burn.

Afterword

If you take the Moon Pass road from Wallace down to Avery, you'll see off to your right an occasional snag still standing where it burned in 1910.

If you turn west from Avery and drive the road that parallels where the Milwaukee used to run, you'll eventually reach St. Maries, where two circles of stone in a small cemetery mark the graves of many of the firefighters who died fighting the Big Burn. Some of the stones have names on them. Others have just a date and place—Setzer Creek, Slate Creek, Big Creek.

The snags and the memorials tell stories of land and individuals caught and forever changed by events beyond anyone's control. Close to ninety people died. A good part of Wallace was reduced to rubble, and several smaller towns were wholly or partially destroyed.

Two and a half million acres of public forest land burned in the Northwest that summer, most of it in the blowup that began on August 20. And that's a measurement made without consideration for the steep landscapes of the burned area. If you flattened out Idaho's mountains—turned their vertical heights into a flat, horizontal acreage—you'd have a state larger than Texas.

And that two and a half million acres doesn't count all the private land that burned.

It's no wonder that if you talk long enough to anyone who knows fire or Forest Service history, sooner or later you'll hear about the Big Burn. They'll assume you know where they mean and when it happened. And that you'll understand, too, why, for decades, memories of it would influence how foresters thought about fire and fire fighting.

———◆———

As I write this we are approaching the end of a droughty summer, and fire crews are stretched thin across Washington, Idaho, and Montana. Across the Northwest, hot days last week paired with nights of dry lightning. Winds that moved in ahead of a cold front fanned embers into flames and spotted fires across hand lines and fuel breaks.

I can hear the growl of an air tanker flying overhead. It's carrying fire retardant from the aerial depot west of Missoula to dump in front of a wildfire burning in the Seeley Lake Ranger District, where my son, Kurt, has a summer job on a Forest Service fire crew.

Kurt's not anywhere near the Seeley Lake fire, however. Instead, he's over in Idaho, part of a twenty-person crew sent to help fight wildfire on land burned in the summer of 1910. And, probably, several times since.

Fortunately, the parallel pretty much ends with the place, a loose similarity in weather, and the time of year.

For Kurt is not Jarrett, going into an unknown situation, without protective clothing, untrained except for a few instructions from a big brother and a fireline friend. Kurt wears fire-resistant Nomex clothing—olive pants, a long-sleeved, bright yellow shirt. He wears a hard hat, gloves, high boots. Sometimes he filters air through a dry bandanna.

He frequently uses a chain saw, but his favorite tool is a Pulaski. Part ax, part hoe, it's named for the man who perfected it—the same Ed Pulaski who was a ranger on the Coeur d'Alene in 1910.

Kurt also wears a fire pack that stays with him when he's on the line—he could lose his job if he were caught without it. Inside are flares called fusees, brightly colored flagging for marking trails and hazard trees, a two-way radio, a first-aid kit, a fireline handbook, a file for keeping tools sharp, food, and a gallon and a half of water. And, most important, a heat-resistant shelter. It looks like a brick of accordion-pleated foil. Opened out, crawled under, anchored down with feet and hands, it could save his life in a blowup.

And he's trained. He attended classes to get his red card— the required ticket to a job fighting forest fires—while still in high school. Then, before his first fire assignment, the Forest Service put him through days of training, conditioning, and certifications. And at the start of each fire season, he and his crewmates retake a class called Standards for Survival, learning again about the "watch out" situations—the situations that have led to accidents and tragedies, and that nobody wants to repeat.

Because, despite the many great advantages that today's

firefighters have over those of earlier years, when they go on a fire, they go in harm's way. Fire fighting remains a very hazardous job, and hardly a year passes that wildfire doesn't claim at least one life.

That more aren't lost is in large part due to lessons learned, sacrifices made, and memories forged, going back to the Big Burn and coming forward to today. It's a heritage renewed every time a firefighter goes out to meet fire.

Jeanette Ingold

Missoula, Montana

August 20, 2001

Acknowledgments

◆

I'm indebted to many people for helping me understand the forces—fire, weather, people, institutions—that combined strengths or collided when the disastrous forest fires of 1910 swept across northern Idaho and western Montana. I was also fortunate in having a wealth of written material to draw upon in my research, and I've put into the suggested readings list several of the published sources that I found especially helpful and that might be good starting places for anyone interested in learning more.

One wonderful source, not readily available in its entirety, is the four-volume *Early Days in the Forest Service,* a collection of memoirs of early foresters compiled by the U.S. Forest Service in the 1940s and selectively republished in *"I'll Never Fight Fire with My Bare Hands Again": Recollections of the First Forest Rangers of the Inland Northwest.* The section contributed by William W. Morris contains "The Great Fires of 1910," a piece about his experiences as a young ranger that fateful summer, beginning with his trip up Striped Peak, an account that I drew on to begin this book.

Another Forest Service publication, *When the Mountains Roared: Stories of the 1910 Fires* by Elers Koch, supervisor of Montana's Bitterroot National Forest that summer, recounts the experiences of several rangers caught in the blowup and places them within the framework of the fire season's progression and aftermath.

Among newer publications, Stephen J. Pyne's *Year of the Fires: The Story of the Great Fires of 1910* brings together a huge amount of information about the 1910 fire season and the events of the blowup, and examines them within a larger context of fire and Forest Service history.

Contemporaneous local newspapers are always one of my favorite sources for the historical details and voices of a particular time and place, and in researching this book I found the July through September 1910 issues of the weekly *Idaho Press* invaluable. I'm grateful to the Wallace Public Library for making them available on microfilm. Great help also came from the librarians and collections at the University of Montana Mansfield Library and at the public libraries in Missoula and in Spokane, Washington.

I'm indebted to Dr. Richard Hutto of the University of Montana for sharing his knowledge of the regeneration that occurs in burned forests.

Forest Service people have been generous with their help, and I'd like especially to thank David Asleson, Amanda Burbank, Cort Sims, and David Stack. And thanks go, too, to those who helped me with historical details— John Amonson, Kermit Edmonds, Jason Patent, and L. J. Richards.

Others that I'm very grateful to for their guidance and critical reading are my good friends Wendy Norgaard, Dorothy Hinshaw Patent, Peggy Christian, and Dr. Ted; my son, Kurt; and my husband, whom I can always count on to bring fresh eyes to a project.

Sources and Suggestions
for Further Reading

THE U.S. FOREST SERVICE AND FIREFIGHTERS, YESTERDAY AND TODAY

Books

Beil, Karen Magnuson. *Fire in Their Eyes: Wildfires and the People Who Fight Them.* San Diego: Harcourt, 1999.

Guthrie, C. W., ed., with additional material by C. W. Guthrie, Jean Liebig Soldowski, and Don Bunger. *The First Ranger: The Stories of Frank Liebig and Fred Herrig.* Huson, Mont.: Redwing, 1995.

Rothman, Hal K., ed. *"I'll Never Fight Fire with My Bare Hands Again": Recollections of the First Forest Rangers of the Inland Northwest.* Lawrence, Kan.: University Press of Kansas, 1994.

Taylor, Murry A. *Jumping Fire: A Smokejumper's Memoir of Fighting Wildfire.* New York: Harcourt, 2000.

Internet Sources

Idaho Panhandle National Forests home page.
http://www.fs.fed.us/ipnf

Lolo National Forest main page. Describes forest life after a fire.
http://www.fs.fed.us/r1/lolo/wl-fire-ecology/fire1.html

National Interagency Fire Center (Boise, Idaho) home page.
http://www.nifc.gov

U.S.D.A. Forest Service home page.
http://www.fs.fed.us

1910 FIRES

Books

Cohen, Stan, and Don Miller. *The Big Burn: The Northwest's Great Forest Fire of 1910.* Rev. ed. Missoula, Mont.: Pictorial Histories, 1993.

Koch, Elers. *When the Mountains Roared: Stories of the 1910 Fires.* Missoula, Mont.: U.S. Department of Agriculture Forest Service, 1944.

Morris, William W. *The Great Fires of 1910.* Vol. 1 of *Early Days in the Forest Service.* Missoula, Mont.: U.S. Department of Agriculture Forest Service, 1944.

Pyne, Stephen J. *Year of the Fires: The Story of the Great Fires of 1910.* New York: Viking Penguin, 2001.

Spencer, Betty Goodwin. *The Big Blowup: The Northwest's Great Fire.* Caldwell, Idaho: Caxton Printers, 1956.

Newspaper

The Idaho Press. Wallace, Idaho. July–September, 1910.

1910 LIFE BETWEEN THE ST. JOE AND COEUR D'ALENE RIVERS

Books

Crowell, Sandra A., and David O. Asleson. *Up the Swiftwater: A Pictorial History of the Colorful Upper St. Joe River Country.* Rev. ed. Coeur d'Alene, Idaho: Museum of North Idaho, in cooperation with Sandra A. Crowell and David O. Asleson, 1995.

Johnson, Stanley W. *The Milwaukee Road in Idaho: A Guide to Sites and Locations.* Coeur d'Alene, Idaho: Museum of North Idaho, 1997.

THE TWENTY-FIFTH INFANTRY

Books

Bailey, Linda C. *Fort Missoula's Military Cyclists: The Story of the 25th U.S. Infantry Bicycle Corps.* Missoula, Mont.: The Friends of the Historical Museum at Fort Missoula, 1997.

Meyer, Bette Eunice. *Fort George Wright: Not Only Where the Band Played: A Historical Geography.* Fairfield, Wash.: Ye Galleon Press, 1994.

Nankivell, John H., comp. and ed. *Buffalo Soldier Regiment: History of the Twenty-fifth United States Infantry, 1869–1926.* 1927. Reprint, Fort Collins, Colo.: Old Army Press, 1972.

Sorensen, George Niels. *Iron Riders: Story of the 1890s Fort Missoula Buffalo Soldiers Bicycle Corps.* Missoula, Mont.: Pictorial Histories, 2000.

Internet Source

U.S. Army Center of Military History home page. http://www.army.mil/cmh-pg/